"Guxx Unfufadoo, concernéd demon,
Asks you why you read quotations,
When you know Wuntvor's in danger;
Says you should get on with this book!"
> —The preceding was provided by
> The Equal Time for Demons Act,
> Vushta common law #77034
> (recently repealed).

"Gardner skewers all the cliches of quest-fantasy with wit, style, mordant irony and great glee—this series could have been serialized in *National Lampoon*, or filmed by one of the Pythons!"
> —Spider Robinson

"The field needs more humorists of this caliber!"
> —Robert Asprin

"Gardner has a fine sense of just when to deflate an apparent threat into slapstick."
> —*Newsday*

Ace Books by Craig Shaw Gardner

The Ebenezum Trilogy

A MALADY OF MAGICKS
A MULTITUDE OF MONSTERS
A NIGHT IN THE NETHERHELLS

A DIFFICULTY WITH DWARVES
AN EXCESS OF ENCHANTMENTS

AN EXCESS OF ENCHANTMENTS

Craig Shaw Gardner

ACE BOOKS, NEW YORK

To Heather,
who likes this sort of thing...

ONE

"Things are not always what they seem."

> —Words (which some expected to be his
> last) spoken by Ebenezum, greatest
> wizard of the Western Kingdoms, when he
> was discovered in close and personal
> consultation with Queen Vivazia of
> Humboldt by the queen's husband, King
> Snerdlot the Vengeful. Unfortunately,
> the following statements made by the
> king to his elite assassin guards, as
> well as the reply uttered by the wizard
> as he climbed down the battlements of
> Humboldt castle in his nightshirt,
> have been lost to posterity.

Once upon a time, in a land very, very far away, there traveled
a young lad who wanted to see the world. Now this lad's name
was Wuntvor, and he wished to be an adventurer and visit that
distant place from which every morning came the sun. As he
grew toward manhood, he would look out his bedroom window

each dawn as he awoke, and watch the sun rise. He began to think of it as his friend, and he imagined the blazing orb beckoned to him, calling Wuntvor to come and see its home.

So it was that Wuntvor left his native land and journeyed east. He walked for many days, until the days turned into weeks, but Wuntvor did not despair, for he was young and his heart was pure. The weeks became months, and still Wuntvor traveled on, for, although the sun seemed no closer than when he started, he knew that if he but tried hard enough and long enough, he would reach his goal.

Still, the way was long and tiring, with hills and mountains to climb and rivers and oceans to cross. Even one as young and pure of heart as Wuntvor found himself doubting the wisdom of his journey from time to time. So it was on a particular evening, when the sun had journeyed all the way from its home in the east to its resting place in the west. Wuntvor was weary from his day's march, and decided to camp in a secluded glen by the side of a babbling brook. He spread out his bedroll and ate a meagre meal of bread and cheese, listening to the nightbirds overhead.

"Alas," he said at last, more to himself than to the birds. "Will I never find the home of the sun?"

And a voice answered him:

"Why ever would you want to do that?"

Wuntvor started, realizing that the voice came from a small man who stood by his knee. After he caught his breath, Wuntvor answered:

"It is what I have always dreamed of. It is my heart's desire."

"Really?" said the small man, who was dressed all in brown and sported a pair of translucent brown wings. "Well then, you have come to the right place."

"And just what place have I come to?" Wuntvor inquired.

"Why," the little fellow said with a big smile, "you have come to f-f-fairyland—" He had quite some difficulty pronouncing the word. "—of course."

"Of course," Wuntvor agreed. "And if this is fairyland, who are you?"

"Why, I am—" The little fellow paused and frowned. "If this is f-f-f-fair-fairyland—" The fellow paused again. His face had turned a bright blue. He took a breath and resumed his speech. "If this is—uh—that place, then I must be a f-f—" His two tiny fists shot into the air. "I am no such thing. I am a Brownie! And proud of it! More than proud! In smallness there is greatness! Brownies forever!"

Wuntvor blinked. Something was wrong here. An old lady stormed down the hill. She did not look happy.

It was then that I remembered where I was.

"No! No! No!" the old lady screamed.

I was in the Eastern Kingdoms, but I had not come here to follow the sun. Rather, I was on a mission of some sort, sent here by my master, the great wizard Ebenezum. Unfortunately, several things had gone wrong. I remembered that, also.

"Can't you even get a simple fairy tale straight?" the old lady demanded. I recognized her now! Her name was Mother Duck. And she was the reason I had been sent to the Eastern Kingdoms!

"I beg your pardon," the small fellow in brown said drily. I knew this person too! His name was Tap! It was all coming back to me at once, as if I had just awoken from a dream.

The little fellow added:

"I do not do fairy tales."

"Is that so?" the old woman queried, her index finger stabbing at the wee man. "No one talks that way to Mother Duck!"

The little fellow took a step back as he hesitantly replied, "I—I would do a Brownie tale!"

"Would you now?" Mother Duck replied. "Well, this is my kingdom and these are my stories. And what we do in this kingdom is make up fairy tales—whether you like it or not. You'll become a part of my stories, and you will like it!" Her mouth twisted into a cruel grin. "We'll just have to make the spell a little stronger."

"Never!" the Brownie bravely retorted. "No spell is as strong as Brownie pride!"

"We'll see." Mother Duck stared intently at the little fellow.

"I am sorry," Tap insisted, doing his best to ignore the old lady's stare, "but I am a Brownie, and will be until my—uh, that is—I am—uh, aren't I—um—welcome to fairyland, home of the happy-go-lucky fairies! Like me!"

Tap tried to perform a happy-go-lucky skip, with little success. He didn't look happy at all.

"Very well," Mother Duck remarked with a heavy sigh. "That's one problem taken care of." She regarded me critically. "I trust you are going to be cooperative?" She turned her gaze from me to look to the heavens. "Why must I suffer so for my art? Why can't they understand what I'm trying to create?"

I didn't know what to do. I remembered now that I had been sent here by my master to try to win Mother Duck over to our side in the war with the demons of the Netherhells, who were using their fearsome Conquest by Committee in an attempt to take over the surface world. However, once we had arrived in the Eastern Kingdoms, we learned from one of our allies, His Brownieship, King of all the Brownies, that Mother Duck had already signed a pact with our enemies.

Unfortunately, it had been too late to escape. We were captured, and I was carried away by a clumsy giant named Richard to take part in something Mother Duck called her "Storybook." Was that where I was now? I had seen Tap the Brownie, but what had happened to my other companions? This Storybook didn't seem so bad. There must be some way to escape, some way to . . .

I looked up to see Mother Duck staring at me. My mouth opened of its own volition, and I began to speak words over which I had no control.

"Once upon a time," my mouth said, and again: "Once upon a time."

"Excuse me," a deep voice sounded from behind me.

I blinked. My mouth snapped shut. The spell was broken.

"What is it?" Mother Duck demanded. "Can't you see I'm creating?"

"Sorry," the voice said. "I was looking for Mother Duck."

"Well, you've found her!" The woman's tone was filled with rage.

"Oh," the voice replied. "So pleased to meet you."

I tore my eyes away from Mother Duck and turned to regard the newcomer. He was not at all what I expected. For one thing, he was totally covered with thick brown hair. For another, he appeared to be built like an animal, although he was standing on his hind legs. He wore no clothes, save for a green cap inscribed with the words: "Do it again, Celtics!" If I didn't know better, I would have sworn this creature was more animal than human. In fact, I would have sworn he was—

"My name is Wolf," the hairy newcomer said.

Exactly.

"I can see that," Mother Duck replied. Her anger seemed to have abated somewhat. Even she was taken aback by the animal's manner.

"Jeffrey Wolf, to be precise," the newcomer continued rapidly. "And I think *you'll* be glad you met me."

"I certainly hope so," Mother Duck said, "for your sake."

"For *both* our sakes," Jeffrey replied smoothly. "I trust I've come to the right place. You *are* the Mother Duck who does fairy tales?"

The old woman laughed through her nose. "No one else would dare to call themselves Mother Duck."

"Quite assuredly." Jeffrey smiled, showing two rows of very sharp teeth. "I like a woman who knows who she is and what she wants. And what you need in your fairy tales is a talking wolf! Just think of it! What an opportunity!"

"Possibly," Mother Duck agreed, slowly. "I won't kill you just yet, then. A talking wolf? Not as good as an Eternal Apprentice, but I suppose it does have possibilities."

The Eternal Apprentice! The words came rushing at me with the force of a winter wind in July. So there were still other things I had yet to remember. Like the fact that I had met Death on my way to the Eastern Kingdoms, and he had called me the Eternal Apprentice, a person destined to always aid heroes, a person who furthermore was clumsy but lovable, and who was always accompanied by any number of companions. And the dread apparition also told me that this apprentice was someone who could not truly die, but instead, as soon as his earthly body expired, would be reborn into another body, so that his soul would always be free from Death. Unless, of course, Death caught that person alone and snatched that person in that instant to his grave.

I remembered now how barely I had escaped the foul fiend.

What else had I forgotten from my past? And if this Eternal Apprentice thing was true, how did I know that Death would not come and snatch me while I was under one of Mother Duck's spells?

I could not let this woman control me again. I would have to escape, and somehow reunite with my other companions. But how could I get away? We seemed to be surrounded by forest. I realized I had no idea quite where I was. I would have to wait, and hope that something Mother Duck said would give me a clue.

"I'm glad you see how valuable a talking wolf could be!" Jeffrey said when Mother Duck stopped scowling. "When do I start work?"

"What?" Mother Duck demanded. "When do you start work? As soon as I decide that I shouldn't have the giants carry you away to bake you in their bread!"

"But, madam!" Jeffrey waved both his forepaws, entreating the old woman to listen to reason. "I'm the opportunity of a lifetime! Think of it! A talking wolf! What symbolism! What possibility for metaphor!"

"What an ingredient for the giants' bakery," Mother Duck replied summarily. "Richard!" she shouted. "Oh, Richard!"

I heard a rumbling in the distance. I had hoped to somehow escape while Mother Duck and the wolf argued. But Richard had captured me before. I knew there was nowhere I could run where the giant would not find me again.

The rumbling grew closer and louder, so that I discerned that it was really two noises, one a repeated pounding, as if someone was dropping Bog Womblers from a great height to fall upon the earth below. The second noise was a repeated crashing, as Richard accidentally crushed everything in the vicinity of his path.

The wolf did not look at all happy about this turn of events. "Who," he inquired, somewhat hysterically, "is Richard?"

"Oops!" a great voice declared from high overhead. Richard had arrived.

"Richard?" Mother Duck inquired of her very large lackey.

"I'm sorry I asked," the wolf moaned. "I'll just be going—"

"I hope you didn't need that cottage back there," Richard

pleaded. "It was right next to that muddy river bank, and my foot slipped ever so slightly—"

"Don't worry about it, Richard," interrupted Mother Duck, her voice tinged with fatigue. "I can have the dwarves build another. In the meantime, I have a job for you."

"Let's not be hasty, now," Jeffrey interjected. "I have too great a talent to be baked away!"

"You also have too big a mouth." Mother Duck pointed at Jeffrey. "Richard, make sure the wolf stays quiet while I work. If not—"

The giant grinned. "Whole wolf bread."

"Exactly," the old lady agreed. "Understand. I must have silence when I create! Now—" She paused to look at me.

What could I say? There must be some way to keep from coming under her spell again. What would my master have done? Argued with her, probably. Attempted to get her to see reason. Very well, that was what I would have to do as well. I opened my mouth. "Indeed—," I began.

But the next words that came out were, "Once upon a time."

Once upon a time. Once upon a time.

TWO

"There are two sides to every issue."

> —Words (which some were surprised he
> was still alive to speak) uttered by
> Ebenezum the Wizard to the elite
> assassin guards of King Snerdlot the
> Vengeful, after the king decided to
> question the parentage of some of his
> offspring by Queen Vivazia, who did have
> a habit of long and personal
> consultations with gentlemen wearing
> wizard's robes. Few realize, however,
> that the fleeing Ebenezum was at the
> time disguised as a costermonger
> (although on closer inspection his garb
> might have passed for a wizard's
> nightshirt), and furthermore, that he
> managed to cast Gleebzum's Spell of
> Universal Guilt among the assassins,
> which caused them to spend the rest of that afternoon
> repeatedly arresting each other.

*   *   *

9

Once upon a time, a young lad named Wuntvor traveled far from his native land, seeing the sights and having many adventures. So it was that he came over a hill and saw a bright and verdant valley spread before him. Brilliant sunlight shone down on green trees and golden crops, and Wuntvor thought that he had never seen a place as beautiful as this in all his travels.

He left the hilltop and began his descent into the valley. But he had not gone a dozen paces before he saw a handpainted sign hanging from one of the beautiful, green trees. And on that sign, in large red letters, someone had painted a single word: DANGER.

Wuntvor paused for a moment, and stared at the sign. Was someone trying to warn him? But danger of what? And where could any danger be on such a fine day as this?

So Wuntvor continued upon his way, whistling merrily as he studied the wildflowers that bordered the path on either side. He came to a broad field of wild grass and clover, and saw that on the far side of that field wound a lazy blue river.

Wuntvor looked along the trail he followed, and noted that in the distance it led to a narrow bridge that crossed the wide expanse of water. Well then, he thought to himself, that is the way that I must go. But he had not walked a dozen paces before he found that a giant boulder blocked his way. And on that boulder was painted a single word, in red letters three feet high: BEWARE.

Wuntvor paused for a long moment to regard the message on the boulder. This was the second warning he had received since he had entered the valley. But what were these messages trying to tell him? What, or whom, should he beware of?

At length, Wuntvor decided that it was much too fine a day to beware of anything. Let the fates do what they must, he thought. On a sunny afternoon like this, he could best whatever was thrown in his path!

And with that, Wuntvor skirted the boulder and continued down the trail to the bridge. He had not gone a dozen paces, however, before a large man stepped out from behind a concealing hedge. Wuntvor studied the newcomer with some surprise, since he was the largest man the young lad had ever seen, being massive in girth as well as height. The large fellow was dressed in a bronze breastplate, which was somewhat dented and tarnished, and wore an elaborate winged helmet on top of his massive head. He raised a giant club above his head, and uttered but a single word:

"DOOM."

Wuntvor took a step away, being somewhat taken aback by this new turn of events. Was this the danger that the first sign spoke of? Was this what he had to beware of, as the boulder had cautioned? Yet the large man did not attack. Instead, he simply stood there, the giant club still raised above his massive head.

"Pardon?" Wuntvor said after a moment.

"What?" the large man asked.

"I beg your pardon?" Wuntvor expanded.

"Oh," the large man answered. "Doom."

"Yes," Wuntvor prompted. "But what kind of doom?"

"Oh," the large man answered again. "Down at the bridge."

Wuntvor smiled. Now he was getting somewhere! "What about the bridge?"

"Doom," the large man replied.

But Wuntvor wasn't about to give up. "At the bridge?" he prompted again.

The large man nodded his head and lowered his club.

"That's where the danger is?" Wuntvor added. "That's where I have to beware?"

The large man continued to nod.

"But what is the danger?" Wuntvor insisted. "What do I have to beware of?"

"Doom," the large man insisted.

Wuntvor began to despair of ever getting any real answers out of the large fellow. He gazed down the path at the distant bridge. It certainly looked peaceful enough. Just what was this big fellow trying to warn him about? Wuntvor decided he would try to gain a definite answer one more time.

"Indeed," he began, for there was something reassuring to Wuntvor about beginning sentences in this way, "you tell me that my doom waits on yon bridge?"

The large fellow nodded again, smiling that Wuntvor had understood his plea.

"And yet," Wuntvor continued, "there is no way that you might explain to me what that doom is?"

The large fellow shook his head sadly.

"Doom," he agreed.

"Why not?" Wuntvor demanded, upset with this turn of events.

The large fellow looked all around. When he was convinced they were all alone he spoke to Wuntvor in a voice barely above a whisper.

"I am here as a warning," was all he said.

Wuntvor bit his lip so that he would not scream. After he had regained his composure, he asked:

"But can't you at least inform me what you are warning me about?"

"Doom," the large fellow replied sadly.

"Why?" Wuntvor demanded.

"Because that is the way fairy tales work," the large fellow answered.

Wuntvor blinked. Fairy tales? What was this about fairy tales? The lad felt some faint memory stirring at the back of his brain. A word floated toward his consciousness. Mother. Mother what? Of course, now he remem—

"Once upon a time." Wuntvor's lips moved, saying words he could have sworn he never thought. "Once upon a time."

He shook his head violently and stared at the large man again. "Can you tell me nothing about the bridge?"

"Doom," the immense fellow pondered. "Perhaps I can ask you a question or two. Would you by any chance have a good deal of gold?"

At last! Wuntvor thought, I shall get some information.

"No," he answered. "I am but a penniless traveler, out to seek my fortune in the world."

"Doom," the other responded. "Still, all is not yet lost. Are you good at riddles?"

What was this large fellow talking about? "Riddles?" Wuntvor demanded. "What do riddles have to do with anything?"

"Doom," the immense one replied, nodding to himself as if he had confirmed something he'd known all along. "I suggest you turn around and go the other way, unless you fancy yourself as troll fodder."

And with that, the large fellow turned and disappeared behind a sizable hedge.

"Indeed," Wuntvor mumbled to no one in particular. Somehow, he did not feel he had gained much information at all.

But after a moment's thought, Wuntvor decided to go to the bridge anyway. After all, hadn't he left his native land to seek adventure? He had the feeling that this bridge he was approaching, as small and innocent looking as it was, might contain so much adventure that he could return home immediately after crossing it.

He was not a dozen paces from the bridge when he heard a voice.

> "Ho, young traveler!
> We have advice:
> If you want to cross,
> You will pay a price."

And with that, a horrible creature leapt from beneath the bridge and landed less than a dozen paces away from the startled Wuntvor. The creature's skin was a bright shade of yellowish-green, but that was nowhere near as startling as the horrible fact that it wore clothing filled with purple and green checks, not to mention that it held a brown, smoking thing between its teeth.

The creature removed the brown, smoking thing (which was quite foul smelling besides) from between its jaws, and spoke again.

> "Now that you're here
> You won't get old,
> Unless you give
> This troll some gold."

"Indeed," Wuntvor replied. So this, at last, was what he was being warned about. Wuntvor thought, somehow, that he should feel more cheered by finally learning the truth. The truth, though, left something to be desired.

The hideously garbed creature smiled with even more teeth than a creature like that should have, and sauntered toward the lad. Wuntvor decided that what he mostly wished at this precise moment was that the large fellow he had so recently spoken with had been more specific in his details of the danger's exact nature, so that Wuntvor might be currently pursuing his adventures in an entirely different location from where he was at present.

The creature pointed at Wuntvor. More specifically, its sharp yellow claws pointed at Wuntvor's belt as it spoke again.

> "Gold need not be
> My only reward,
> I'll take instead
> Your meagre sword!"

Wuntvor looked down at his belt. He had a sword? It came as a total surprise to him. Shouldn't a person remember if he was wearing a sword?

Well, he reasoned, as long as he had a sword, he might as well defend himself.

"What are you doing?" the sword screamed as Wuntvor yanked it from the scabbard.

The sword spoke! Wuntvor almost dropped the weapon. He definitely should have remembered a sword that could talk. The lad frowned. Something, he thought, is not as it seems.

"I would like an answer," the sword insisted. "As your personal weapon, I think it's the least I deserve."

"Indeed," Wuntvor responded, wishing to grant the magic sword's wishes. "I was merely drawing you forth to slay yon horrible creature."

"Merely?" the sword began, but whatever it had to say next was lost beneath the creature's new rhyme.

> "Ho, young traveler,
> Your valour growing.
> Sad to say,
> I must be going."

*   *   *

And with that, the garishly garbed creature dove under the bridge.

"Merely?" the enchanted blade repeated.

Wuntvor glared at the sword. "Who are you, anyway?"

"Is that a trick question?" the sword responded, a suspicious edge to its voice.

"Nay," Wuntvor insisted, although he doubted, under the circumstances, that he would know a trick question even if he spoke it. "I fear I am under a spell of forgetfulness, and hoped that a magic sword might know the truth."

"Why didn't you say so?" The sword brightened perceptibly. Wuntvor had to shield his eyes not to be blinded by the glow.

"That's exactly what we magic swords are for," the blade continued. "My name is Cuthbert, and I'm a first-class example of sorcerous weaponry. What else do you need to know? Your name is Wuntvor. You do remember that? Good. Do you recall that you are on a quest for your master—Hey!"

The sword screamed as it fell from Wuntvor's hand, which had gone suddenly numb. But the lad had no more thought for his discarded weapon. All he could think of were the words upon his lips.

"Once upon a time," he said. "Once upon a time."

And, as if in answer, he heard a second voice come from beneath the bridge.

> "Ho, young traveler,
> No need to fiddle!
> You'll simply die
> If you miss this riddle."

And with that a second creature leapt onto the path, less than a dozen paces from Wuntvor, who was nowhere near as startled this time, having come somewhat to expect such occurrences. The second monster was a bit different from the first, a tad shorter and more of a putrid gray-green in color. Its clothing was more conservative as well, as it wore dark, almost monastic-looking robes that ballooned around its short body in great folds.

"Riddle?" Wuntvor inquired. This must be the second thing the large fellow warned him about. A riddle that, according to this creature, he could simply die from. Wuntvor suspected the creature was not speaking metaphorically.

The sickly green thing smiled broadly and pulled a piece of parchment from beneath its robes. It read in a clear, high, annoying voice:

> "With this riddle,
> The seeds are sowed:
> Why did the chicken
> Cross the road?"

The monster licked its chops, obviously intending a quick and tasty meal. The lad had a difficult time even thinking about the riddle.

Wait a second. Wuntvor stared hard at the riddling horror. A chicken crossing the road? That wasn't difficult at all. His aged grandmother had told him the answer to that one a thousand times.

"To get to the other side!" Wuntvor shouted triumphantly.

"Get to the other side?" the green thing mused. "Well, I suppose that's possible. Just a moment." The creature reached within its voluminous robes and pulled forth a sheaf of parchment.

"No, no, I'm afraid the answer is as follows—" It cleared its throat and announced portentously:

"A newspaper."

What? Wuntvor thought. What was a newspaper?

"It is not!" the lad insisted angrily. "Everyone knows that chickens cross the road to get to the other side!"

The creature shook its head sadly, reaching within its robes with its free hand to draw out a knife and fork. "Perhaps that sort of thing happens wherever you come from," it answered as it scanned the sheaf of parchments. "I do remember seeing that answer somewhere. Ah, here it is: 'To get to the other side.' I'm afraid though, that it's the answer to another riddle entirely. Uh—here it is—'What's black and white and read all over?' "

"What's black and white and red all over?" Wuntvor repeated.

The creature nodded triumphantly. "To get to the other side!" It paused, waiting for some sign of recognition from the traveler. "You see now, don't you?" it prompted at last. "You see, because it's black and white and read, it has to cross—" The thing paused and stared for a moment at the parchment. "Well, perhaps it is a little difficult to explain. It has to be correct, though. I assure you, Mother Duck uses nothing but the very latest equipment. So there's no chance for a mistake." The thing blinked, as if it couldn't quite believe what it was saying. "Well, not that much of a chance."

Mother Duck? The lad frowned. Where had he heard that name before? And why did he have an almost uncontrollable urge to say "Once upon a time"?

"Other side?" the thing said, more to itself than to Wuntvor. "What kind of stupid—" The creature stopped itself and, after a moment, coughed discreetly. "Well, perhaps, in the very slight chance there was an error, we should give you another opportunity. It's your life at stake, after all." The green thing riffled through the pile of parchment. "Oh, here's the old chestnut about four legs, two legs, three legs. She's got to be kidding. There must be something with a little more verve than that." The creature turned the page. "Let's try this one."

The monster cleared its throat and spoke in a loud, even more annoying voice: "How many elephants can you get into a Volkswagen?"

It paused, staring at the parchment in disbelief. "Where did she get these questions, anyway?" The creature flipped another page, frowning as it quickly read the text. "Let's see. I don't suppose you have any idea what a—'lightbulb' is? I thought as much."

The thing crumpled the parchment in its green claws. "I'm sorry, this is ridiculous. What am I doing in a stupid fairy tale, anyway?"

Fairy tale? Wuntvor remembered the Brownie. And that woman the thing had mentioned. What was her name? Mother something. It was on the tip of his tongue. Mother—

He had it!

"Once upon a time!" Wuntvor cried in triumph. Wait a second. That wasn't the point he was going to make. Was it?

"Once upon a time," he said again for good measure.

And again, as if in answer, a third voice, far gruffer than either of those that spoke before, came from beneath the bridge.

> "Ho, young traveler,
> Not yet beaten;
> Prepare yourself now
> To be ea—"

But instead of completing the rhyme, the third creature began to sneeze.

"Are you just going to leave me here?" the sword demanded.

The sword? The sword! He looked down to where he had dropped it. Somehow, Wuntvor had forgotten all about the magic weapon again.

"Yeah!" the green thing shouted at Wuntvor. "And just what are we doing in this stupid fairy tale when we're supposed to be on a quest?"

A small brown fellow appeared by the lad's foot. "I couldn't agree more! Fairy tales! Just think how much better it would be if it were a Brownie tale!"

The green thing had recoiled at the very sight of the little fellow. "Don't ever agree with me!" he shouted, then looked back to Wuntvor. "There are simply certain things I cannot cope with."

"I suppose I'm just going to lay in the dust forever," the sword moaned, "left here to rust, forgotten by my owner—"

The checkered monster was suddenly in their midst. "Are you tired of your lot in life, enchanted sword? Well, come with me, and I'll offer you foreign sights, adventure—"

"It's ruined! It's ruined!" a woman's voice called from somewhere far up the hill.

Wait a second, Wuntvor thought.

There was something about all this chaos that was disturbingly familiar. He looked around and remembered that the robed creature was Snarks, a demon who was forced to speak nothing but the truth, no matter how unpleasant that truth might be.

And there, in his checkered suit, was Brax the traveling Salesdemon, purveyor of previously owned enchanted weapons, "Every one a Creampuff!" And the sword was Cuthbert, a weapon that was unfortunately a bit of a coward. And he had seen Tap the Brownie during his last fairy tale.

His last fairy tale?

That's right! He was a prisoner of Mother Duck, who was currently storming down the hill toward them, pursued by a hairy fellow who looked rather like a wolf standing on his hind legs, sporting a green cap. Hadn't he seen this fellow before somewhere, too? Wuntvor shook his head.

I wondered what else I didn't remember.

Somebody was sneezing, but it didn't sound like my master. A large, blueish-purple, and quite horrible creature crawled from a ravine beneath the nearby bridge. It grabbed a corner of Brax's sportcoat and blew its nose.

> "Guxx Unfufadoo, noble demon,
> Wants no more of fairy stories!
> Will no longer obey Mother;
> Will turn Mother into ducklings!"

"Is that so?" Mother Duck replied drily. "And what seems to have upset my little demon so?"

Guxx advanced on the old lady, his talons spread wide, ready to rip and shred. As he lifted his claws above the woman to prepare for the kill, he uttered three final words:

"No more poetry."

THREE

The wise wizard should, if at all possible, avoid making plans during a crisis. The only problem with this advice is that the mage often discovers that the crisis has already made plans for the wise wizard.

—The Teachings of Ebenezum,
VOLUME VII

Guxx advanced on Mother Duck.

The old woman stood her ground. "Don't you think for a minute that you can defeat me. Once upon—"

"Did I hear someone mention poetry?" a booming voice called from the direction of the bridge. I turned away from Guxx to see Hubert the dragon landing in the river, the beautiful Alea astride his broad blue back. But wasn't there something different about the damsel? Perhaps it was that she was wearing a new gown of royal blue. Then again, I did not remember her blond tresses as being so long that they covered most of the dragon's back.

Still, all this fairy tale business seemed to be jumbling my memory. At that moment, I could not swear to anything.

"We'll give you something better than poetry!" the dragon called. "Hit it, Damsel!"

The beautiful Alea sang in a clear, high voice:

> "All your troubles don't mean a thing,
>   Whether you're rich, whether you're poor;
> Forget your troubles and dance and sing,
>   For Damsel and Dragon are the cure!"

With that, she did an impromptu dance across Hubert's scales as the dragon beat time with his wings.

"If they're the cure," Snarks mumbled, "give me the disease."

"What are you two doing here?" Mother Duck demanded, forgetting Guxx to concentrate on the new arrivals. "You were supposed to wait on the other side of the bridge!"

"We were?" the dragon asked. "Well, why didn't someone tell us about this? We *can* take direction when required. We're theater people, you know."

"Well, I was going to give you the role of your careers!" Mother Duck seemed to be getting upset. "You were going to be the climax of the fairy tale!"

"Oh, is that what we were doing?" Hubert laughed apologetically. "I was wondering about that. I mean, for some reason, there we were, humming this idiotic ditty about 'Once upon a time, once upon a time.' Then—zap!—we suddenly remembered who we were and what we were doing here, and next thing we knew, there was this tremendous commotion outside. What could we do but investigate?"

"That's right!" Alea chorused. "Damsel and Dragon are always where the action is!"

"Well, this time you'll wish you were where the action wasn't!" Mother Duck raised her hands above her head. Was she going to conjure?

Guxx leapt for her with a roar.

It all happened so quickly, I wasn't quite sure what had transpired. One minute, the heavily muscled demon was flying through the air, straight toward the old lady. Just as his sharp and deadly claws were about to reach Mother Duck, however, the demon somehow managed to perform a complete somersault in midair and land on his back in the mud at the river's edge.

"Must we be tiresome?" Mother Duck murmured. "I could eat demons like you for lunch. Why do you think the Netherhells were forced to sign a pact with me?"

A chill ran through my frame as I remembered the true severity of our situation. Not only were we prisoners of this woman, but Mother Duck had already allied herself with the evil forces of the Netherhells, a demonic horde who wished to control the surface world for their own foul purposes. My fellow questers and I had been sent to try to enlist Mother Duck in our cause by my master and his fellow wizards of Vushta, now all afflicted with a dread malady that caused them to sneeze whenever confronted by sorcery. This malady made them easy prey for the magical might of the Netherhells, and it appeared that all might be lost for the surface world unless we might gain the aid of the mysterious woman who controlled the Eastern Kingdoms. Once we had met this woman, though, we discovered that Mother Duck had already allied herself with the forces of darkness.

Was there no hope, then, of saving Vushta and the rest of the surface world from an eternity of Netherhells domination? I choked back a cry of anguish. If I foundered in despair, all would be lost.

Indeed, I thought to myself, trying to calm my fears enough to rationally deal with the problem. How would my master, the great wizard Ebenezum, handle a situation like this?

That was easy. I knew he would have continued with his noble purpose, no matter what the odds. There was only one answer, then. As difficult as it appeared, I had to somehow find a way to get Mother Duck to change her mind.

"Indeed!" I called out to Mother Duck, who was still glowering at the mud-covered Guxx. "I was wondering if we might talk about this pact of yours."

"Eh?" The woman glanced at me as one might regard a passing insect. "Ah. The Eternal Apprentice. Now, now, don't worry your mythic little head about those things. Mother Duck knows what's best for you."

"Indeed?" I replied, rather taken aback. Mythic little head? This was going to be more difficult than I thought.

Guxx pointed a claw at Brax the Salesdemon, who had managed to help his fellow creature rise from the mud.

"Begin!" Guxx exclaimed. Brax began to beat on a drum that he fished out of a sack he had been carrying over his shoulder.

> "Guxx Unfufadoo, muddy demon,
> Follows Wuntvor, noble quester,
> You will listen to the 'prentice,
> Or you will feel Guxx's fury!"

The large demon cracked his massive knuckles for emphasis.

Mother Duck yawned. "Must we continue to be so tiresome? No one needs to feel anybody else's fury. We're here to make fairy tales."

The hairy fellow with the green cap trotted over to the old woman. "And speaking of fairy tales, may I say that I can see any number of ways to improve your presentation?"

Mother Duck stared glumly at the hairy fellow. She seemed a bit out of sorts.

"Ahem," the hairy fellow replied, glancing at me and doffing his cap. "Pardon me, but I don't think we've been introduced. Wolf's the name. Jeffrey Wolf."

I began to introduce myself in turn when I was interrupted by the very loud noise of Hubert emerging from the lake.

"But you haven't had a chance to see our act!" the dragon called to Mother Duck. "Now, however, that you have dealt with that untimely interruption, it's time to begin!" The trees shook as Hubert tap-danced his way into our midst.

Mother Duck stared at no one in particular. "What have I done to deserve this?"

"I've asked myself the same question a thousand times," Snarks confided in the old woman.

"Shall we tell them about our new dance craze?" Alea piped up.

"That'll wow them!" the dragon agreed. "Ah-one and ah-two—"

Alea jumped from the dragon's back, careful to sweep her incredibly long hair aside so that it wouldn't get in her way. The two began to sing:

*   *   *

"Don't you act so nonchalant,
Let's both go where the dancing's hot!
Cause you can go wherever you want
When you're doing the Dragon Trot!"

Mother Duck regarded the performers, all the color drained from her face. "All I want to do is create," she moaned. "And now this."

Damsel and Dragon continued:

"First you fling your right foot, fast and free;
You might crush a bush, you might crush a tree.
Then you kick your left foot, what a romp;
And if they don't like it— Stomp! Stomp! Stomp!"

Damsel and Dragon crushed a large amount of underbrush under foot for emphasis before they launched once again into the chorus:

"Don't you act so nonchalant,
Let's both go where the dancing's hot!
Cause you can go—"

"Twenty-three years," Mother Duck went on. "I've been doing this for twenty-three years, and never, ever . . ." Her voice died before she could finish the sentence. Alea began to dance between the dragon's toes, as, high above her, Hubert performed selected birdsong imitations.

Mother Duck shook her head. "My dear mother always told me I should go into another line of work. You'll never go hungry if you become a General Witch Practitioner, she'd always say. And love potions! You can get rich with love potions! But no. I had to follow my own muse and get involved with characters like this."

Damsel and Dragon launched into yet another verse:

"Next you take your tail and swish it around;
Be sure to flatten everything down to the ground;
What you can't stomp down you can certainly push.
Say, hey, you're a dragon so crush! Crush! Crush!"

*   *   *

Guxx Unfufadoo began to sneeze.

Mother Duck looked about her entreatingly, as if, somewhere in her Eastern Kingdoms, there might be something that would enable everything to make sense. It was an amazing transformation. This once strong woman, the mistress of all she surveyed, suddenly looked like a tourist lost without her guidebook. A moment ago, she had flicked Guxx Unfufadoo away as if the demon lord were some insignificant gnat. Now, Damsel and Dragon seemed to have totally undone her.

Not that I hadn't seen it happen before. As the demon Snarks might say, when you watched Damsel and Dragon perform, it was like giving a whole new definition to the word "entertainment." Faced with an act of Damsel and Dragon's character, Mother Duck didn't have a chance.

Still, it was an amazing transformation. Perhaps this would be a good time to make my proposal.

"Indeed," I began as the duo launched into another chorus. "I was wondering—"

"Where have I gone wrong?" Mother Duck asked, turning to face me. "I'll be honest with you, I've never felt quite comfortable with the whole thing from the very beginning. Even my name—Mother Duck. Oh, it's not a bad name, mind you, but it doesn't have quite the snap I was looking for. If your fairy tales are going to be remembered throughout history, your name should have some snap. Don't you agree?"

"Uh, —" I answered. "I suppose so. But I wanted to talk about Vushta—"

"What about something more regal," the old woman suggested, "like Mother Swan?"

"Very nice," I replied rapidly, "but about your pact with the Nether—"

Mother Duck wrinkled her nose and shook her head. "No, a swan's much too fussy. I think it should be a common everyday bird, one that people could relate to. Like Mother Sparrow? No, that's a bit plain. Mother Grackle, maybe?" The old woman made a face, shaking her head as soon as the words had left her mouth.

Damsel and Dragon continued. Did the song have no end?

* * *

"Now you know how to do the Dragon Trot,
It's the best dance craze we ever got!
You know being a dragon is such a joy,
And if they don't like it: Destroy! Destroy!"

Damsel and Dragon ended with a flourish, bowing to everyone gathered in the clearing.

"Over?" Mother Duck whispered. "It's over?"

"Did we hear a disappointed cry in the audience?" Hubert queried. "Is it time for an encore?"

"No! No!" their audience replied en masse.

"Indeed," I added hastily, eager to have them out of the way so that I could get back to my discussion with Mother Duck. "Why ruin a perfect performance by dragging it on needlessly? Rather, let us remember your song for its brilliance and brevity."

Hubert nodded solemnly. "The apprentice has a point."

Mother Duck nodded in turn. "Furthermore," she stated, the power once again in her voice, "if you attempt to sing a song like that again, I will be forced to cast a spell of eternal silence over you." She pointed both her aged but still nimble hands at Hubert. "Think carefully, or you could spend the rest of your life as a silent dragon."

"A spell of silence?" Hubert replied, aghast. "A silent dragon?"

But Alea nodded her head knowingly. "Don't you see?" she told the dragon. "She's never seen actors from the theaters of Vushta before. She's obviously afraid of being upstaged."

"Oh, dear." The dragon sighed in agreement. "It's the price you have to pay when you play the provinces."

"Good," Mother Duck stated. "I'm glad that's settled. I'm afraid I was a bit startled by your first song and dance. I assure you that next time I will be prepared for anything you have to offer." She flexed her conjuring fingers absently. "Remember, the next time I hear the Dragon Trot, you lose your vocal chords."

A solitary smoke ring rose from the stunned dragon's nose. She had done what I thought impossible—rendered Hubert speechless.

Mother Duck allowed herself a smile. She was in a good mood at last. It was time to make my plea!

"Indeed," I began. "Now that you have dealt with that small problem, perhaps we may talk in earnest."

"Hmm?" Mother Duck replied, as if she had forgotten all about me. "Oh, the Eternal Apprentice? Yes, I did rattle on there a bit, didn't I? Well, you shouldn't worry about it. I have quite recovered. In fact, I think it's almost time for our next fairy tale."

"Indeed?" She couldn't leave now! I had been so close. She had to hear me out! "But—"

"Now, now, don't keep interrupting Mother Duck. That's a good myth figure. There's no need to get upset." She smiled condescendingly. "In fact, with what I have planned for you, I think you'll need to conserve your strength."

She stood, hands on hips, and surveyed all who stood around her. "The first two fairy tales didn't work, but I've learned from my mistakes. I was thinking too small. You and your companions keep breaking out of the narrow confines of the tiny stories I have been giving to you. But no more. I am going to concoct a fairy story the equal of all of you." She sighed happily. "With luck, it will be my masterpiece!"

"A worthy goal," Jeffrey the wolf agreed. "But just think how much more resonance your stories would have, not to mention symbolism that might speak to a dozen unborn generations, if your tales featured clever talking wolves?"

Mother Duck sighed. "I've had just about enough outside interference. Maybe I should have Richard take you away after all. I mean, what kind of fairy tale would use a talking wolf?"

"What kind of fairy tale?" Jeffrey emitted a barking laugh. "Listen, lady, I've got some great ones. How about this little kid who has to take this basket of goodies through the woods to her grandmother's house. But the wolf, you see, eats the grandmother and takes her place."

Mother Duck looked at the wolf with new respect. "Really? Well, it does have some interesting elements. I like the kid and the grandmother. A nice family angle. The woods and the goodies aren't bad either. They lend necessary color, I think. And the wolf eating the grandmother gives us that good old fairy tale violence that children love so much. What happens next?"

Jeffrey smiled, pleased with the approval. "Why, I eat the kid, too! Is that great or what?"

"You eat the kid, too?" Mother Duck made a face. "Who would want to hear a fairy tale like that?"

"What do you mean?" Jeffrey replied, somewhat miffed. "It's really popular in the Wolf family."

"It only proves, if you want a good fairy tale, you've got to tell it yourself." And with that, Mother Duck climbed back up the hill. Jeffrey the wolf trotted right behind her.

My hope faded as Mother Duck walked away. I had completely failed in my plea for her to change allegiance. How could I get her to see our side of the issue if she wouldn't even talk to me?

But again, I would not let myself crumble into despair. For my memory was still returning, and, as Mother Duck had surveyed those gathered in the clearing, I had looked around as well. And, as I looked around, I remembered. Here were my companions, Tap the Brownie, Hubert and Alea, and the three demons: Snarks, Guxx and Brax.

And I remembered that I had more companions . . .

First, where had Hendrek gone? The large warrior had appeared in the second fairy tale, warning me of "Doom" if I crossed the bridge. Yet, I had not seen him at all since I had regained my senses. True, Mother Duck might simply have placed him elsewhere, to prepare for the next part of her fairy story. Somehow, though, I wondered, for there were others that I had not seen at all.

One was the vain unicorn, who had followed me all this distance wishing to put its head in my lap. The unicorn, though, had been born in these Eastern Kingdoms. It had known of Mother Duck from before our present quest. Perhaps it also knew a way to avoid her powers. Of course, it could be waiting for me in the next fairy tale as well. So could the Seven Other Dwarves, who could not really be called companions, as we had met them so recently upon our travels, except for the fact that they had tried, unsuccessfully, to protect me from Mother Duck.

I had to face it: it all could be random chance, all controlled in some arcane fashion by the mistress of fairy tales, Mother Duck. Yet, somehow, I sensed a plan behind all these defections, because one more person was absent from this clearing, and had somehow absented herself completely from Mother Duck's spells. This last person gave me hope, for the final fugitive was my beloved, the young witch Norei.

Norei! When I thought of her, everything fell into place. I knew the real reason I had come on this quest. Oh, certainly, I came to save my master, the great wizard Ebenezum, not to mention rescuing the wondrous metropolis of Vushta, city of a thousand forbidden delights, and the entirety of the surface world from the devastating evil of total defeat at the hands of the Netherhells. But I had personal reasons for my quest as well, reasons in their own way as important if not more so than the grand goals we had set out with on the quest to the Eastern Kingdoms. And those reasons could be summarized in one word:

Norei!

She was my *real* reason for being on this quest. But then, she was my real reason for everything. I had met other women before my young witch, had even fancied myself for a brief moment in love with one or two of them. Ah, they had been naught but schoolboy crushes, every one, even my liaison with the lovely Alea before she left the Western Woods to join the theater; but it took meeting a woman like Norei to show me the error of my ways.

So it was that I risked my life in the Eastern Kingdoms. I needed to make the world a safe place for Norei and me to be together, a place where we might, if things were to work out as I hoped, grow old together. True, Norei and I had had a few small misunderstandings when we had been together in Vushta. Oh, nothing insurmountable, I was sure, just a tiny confusion about a meeting or two I had had with Alea, and what small problem I had getting the actress to see that whatever had once been between us was now gone. In fact, I had almost succeeded in this goal, and would have gladly explained the few difficulties that still remained to my beloved Norei, if the young witch had still been talking to me. But, of course, she wasn't, because of an incident with Alea and some canvas, not to mention—but, perhaps it was all a bit too complicated to dwell on at present. I would better spend my time devising some way to contact Norei, for I felt it was only with the aid of the young witch that we would escape Mother Duck's clutches.

But Mother Duck had walked away. My companions and I were alone; beyond her control for the first moment since we had met. Why was I sitting here thinking when I could be acting? I did not know when an opportunity like this would come again. We would have to talk quickly and make plans before the old woman on the hill wove her spells about us once more.

"Indeed!" I called to my fellows. "Gather 'round. We must talk!"

The Brownie, Damsel and Dragon and the three demons all came forward, forming a rough half-circle around me.

"It appears that Mother Duck has left us alone for a moment. We must foment some sort of plan. There is no way we may complete our quest while we are trapped by this woman's power. In addition, we all know the situation in Vushta, with every wizard there sneezing at the mention of sorcery. Each moment we are imprisoned, the forces of the Netherhells are that much closer to victory. What can we do?"

"Perhaps a cheerful song might help," Hubert suggested.

"Then again," Snarks interrupted, "perhaps it might not."

"Begin!" Guxx instructed Brax, who was still holding the drum. Brax beat as Guxx declaimed:

> "Guxx Unfufadoo, noble demon,
>   Will put an end to Netherhells traitors;
>   Will help the 'prentice defeat Mother—"

He glanced at the dragon before continuing:

> "Will put a stop to poetry forever!"

The demon smiled, satisfied he had made his case.

"And I have exactly the right used weapons to do the job!" Brax added.

"Is it time for Brownie Power?" Tap asked.

"Indeed," I replied. "It is time for Brownie Power, and Demon Power, and Damsel and Dragon Power as well. Our strength is in our diversity. We all saw how Mother Duck became a bit undone by the surprise of Hubert and Alea's song. Imagine how shocked she would be if we all used our abilities at the same time?"

"Oh, Wuntie!" Alea exclaimed, rushing over to give me a powerful hug. Her silken blue dress rubbed against my rough shirt, her long blond tresses fell in my face. "How brilliant!" She stepped away to look at me candidly. "I've always wanted to date a genius."

I cleared my throat and looked at the others. Why did the temperature always rise whenever Alea was near?

"Um—er—very well," I continued. "While we still have time, I will quickly outline the plan." I glanced about to make sure I had everyone's attention.

"Now we begin with—uh—we begin—" I was having trouble forming the words. Sweat trickled down my brow. "We—" I tried again. "—Once upon a time."

Alea frowned. "What was that, Wuntie?"

"Oh, no!" Hubert shouted. "I think he's been—he's been—once upon a time."

"You people are making less sense than usual!" Snarks complained. "What's all this—once upon a time?"

"No! It's time for Brownie—" Tap faltered. Both he and Alea said the four words together.

"Once upon a time," Guxx Unfufadoo chimed in. "Once upon a time."

And Brax beat along on his drum.

FOUR

"Here we go again."

—Words (which many were surprised were
not posthumous) spoken by Ebenezum after
he had managed to elude both King Snerdlot
the Vengeful and the monarch's elite
assassin guard by cleverly using the maze
of secret passageways in Snerdlot's
castle, only to open a door to discover
he was once again in the bedchamber of
Queen Vivazia. The queen was, of course,
overjoyed to see him still alive, not to
mention quite hot and sweaty from his
recent pursuit, and therefore
crossed the room in record time to give
the wizard a comradely embrace. Ebenezum
ceased his struggle a moment later, for,
upon reflection, the wizard realized
there were certain things from which
there was truly no escape.

Once upon a time there was a traveler named Wuntvor, who

33

happened upon a little man in the woods.

"Are you a fairy?" Wuntvor asked the little man.

But the little fellow made a face. "Not this time, thank my lucky shoes. No, good sir, I am genuine Brownie, and furthermore, sir, it is your lucky day."

"My lucky day?" Wuntvor said, taken quite by surprise.

"Yes, you're the only other person in this fairy—uh—" The little fellow stopped himself. "—*Brownie* tale, so I guess it has to be you. It *is* your lucky day."

The Brownie stood there, waiting expectantly.

"Thank you," Wuntvor said at last, not knowing what was expected of him.

"Aren't you going to ask why?" the Brownie demanded, tapping his tiny foot.

"Why?" Wuntvor obliged.

"Yes," the Brownie agreed. "*Why* is it your lucky day! Oh, I guess you did ask. Pardon me. My mistake. Performance nerves, I guess. Well, it is your lucky day because you are to be granted seven wishes."

"Seven wishes?" Wuntvor asked.

The Brownie nodded.

"I thought the usual was three," the lad stated.

The Brownie nodded.

"Then why seven?" Wuntvor inquired.

"We're running a special!" the Brownie exclaimed.

"Oh," Wuntvor replied.

"Well, aren't you surprised? Aren't you excited?"

"I guess so," Wuntvor responded, not really sure of anything. He had the nagging feeling that he had been here, or a place very much like here, sometime before.

What was that? Somewhere, in the distance, Wuntvor heard voices arguing. An elderly woman was complaining about how no one understood artists.

"Once upon a time," Wuntvor said. He blinked. "Seven wishes? You're really going to give me seven wishes?" He looked down at the little man in wonder.

"That's more like it," the Brownie replied. "I mean we wee folk expect some enthusiasm for our efforts, you know? That's right, seven wishes for anything you want!"

Anything he wanted? The lad was quite impressed with this

opportunity, although he was the slightest bit scared as well. Seven wishes were a mighty responsibility, and Wuntvor knew all the old stories about farmers and fishermen receiving wishes and squandering them on puddings and the like. He would have to think about this, for he was a young man, abroad to seek his fortune, and this seven wishes thing might be just the chance he was looking for. But, even though he had more than the usual three, Wuntvor knew he would have to use every wish wisely.

"Well," the Brownie said, foot once again tapping. "I'm waiting."

"Uh—" Wuntvor replied in surprise. "I have to start wishing now?"

"Hey, give me a break. You've got seven wishes, here. We Brownies have things to do. Time is shoes, you know!"

Oh, well, Wuntvor thought. Why not? He had to start this wish business some time. He'd have to make the first one a good one.

"Indeed," he began, for that word seemed to help him to think. "I—um—wish I had a stout weapon to protect me from danger."

"Granted!" the Brownie exclaimed.

There was a muffled sound from the direction of his belt, like someone hollering behind a closed door.

"Eh?" Wuntvor said, or a sound very much like that. He looked down, and noticed that there was a sword and scabbard hanging from his belt. The lad grabbed the hilt of the weapon and pulled it free.

"It's about time you let me back out!" the sword exclaimed. "Do you know how boring it can get in there?"

"Pardon?" Wuntvor asked, confused by the weapon's complaint. "About time for what? Have we met before? You are the sword I wished for as the first of my seven wishes. I don't understand what you are talking about."

"First of seven wishes?" the talking sword mused. "Oh, that means we're not still—we're in an entirely different—I see. Excuse me. When you're stuck in a scabbard day in and day out, you lose track of time. I didn't realize we had started another fairy tale."

"It's a Brownie tale!" the little fellow contradicted.

"Wait a minute," Wuntvor interjected. He had been confused from the beginning of this whole thing, and somehow, anything that anybody said to him only seemed to make it worse. He stared at the sword. "You mean you were around here all along?"

"Hey," the Brownie said defensively, "I didn't say you had to wish for something you didn't already have!"

The lad looked open-mouthed at the Brownie. Had the little fellow tricked him?

"You should be more careful with your wishes, you know." The sword chuckled softly to itself. "Before long, I'll bet you'll be wishing for puddings!"

Then he had been tricked, and had had the sword at his belt all along. But why hadn't he remembered the sword? He *had* felt awkward from the first about being in this fairy tale, or Brownie tale, as if he had done something like this before that he could not quite recall. And he hadn't been all that surprised to see the sword at his belt. So maybe he had remembered after all. Or maybe he was remembering that he had remembered it all before.

Wuntvor shook his head. It was very confusing. He simply couldn't remember.

"Well," the Brownie prompted, "we're waiting."

The lad decided he would not let the little fellow fluster him. He didn't know quite how he had gotten the sword, but he had it. This Brownie would cause him to squander his wishes if he wasn't careful.

Wuntvor decided to study his surroundings before he made another wish so as to avoid any more obvious mistakes. He stood at the edge of a bridge over a wide but slow-moving stream. The path wound away from him, up a grassy but steep hill. And on the summit of that hill stood a tower, with but a single window at the very top, a window from which, at this moment, poured thick, gray smoke.

What did this mean? Would his adventures lead him to the smoking tower, or should his fate lead him to the other side of the river? There was something about the bridge, too, that made him the slightest bit uncomfortable, although of course he could not remember exactly what it was, except he could swear it had something to do with poetry.

"Well," the Brownie prompted, "what's it going to be?"

Yes, Wuntvor thought, what was it going to be, the other side of the river or the tower on the hill? He looked again at the sinister gray turbulence roiling from the window above. Actually, if he were to have his preference, he would as soon have all his adventures in places other than smoking towers, thank you.

Well, he'd cross that bridge when he came to it. Or had he crossed it already? The lad glanced back at the river with a frown. If only he could remem—

Wuntvor shook his head sharply, as if he might dislodge any cobwebs that were growing between his ears. Whatever had happened before, it was time to make another wish.

This time he would wish for something a bit more difficult. And something perhaps that was not as dangerous as adventuring to the tower at the top of the hill. And—dare he hope?—something of more lasting importance than any single adventure.

"I wish—" Wuntvor hesitated, wanting to get the words just right. "I wish I could meet a fair damsel to be my own true love."

"Granted!" the Brownie responded cheerfully. "If you'll simply follow me?"

With that, the little fellow started up the hill, toward the smoking tower. The lad glanced up again. Did he see flame shoot through the gray clouds?

"Wait a moment!" Wuntvor exclaimed. "Where are we going?"

"Exactly what I would like to know!" his sword chimed in.

"To meet a fair damsel, just like you wanted. Come on. When you wish for something, you've got to follow through. That's part of the Brownie Code."

"Indeed?" Wuntvor asked, trotting tentatively after the Brownie, who moved very quickly for one so small. "But what if I don't wish to go to the tower?"

The little fellow shook his head. "Sorry, Brownies don't do non-wishes. You'll have to talk to some other magical sub-species about that. Besides, what are you worried about? You still have enough Brownie wishes left to waste one or two."

And with that, the Brownie turned away again and resumed his rapid climb.

Left to waste? Wuntvor wasn't sure he hadn't wasted the two he had already wished. Still, he supposed he'd never know unless he followed the Brownie to the tower. The lad decided to climb the hill.

Smoke still poured from the window. And as he climbed the steep slope, Wuntvor detected a deep rumbling, something he half heard and half felt shaking the ground beneath his feet. What precisely was going on up there?

Wuntvor decided to ask the Brownie.

"Excuse me," he said, increasing his stride to catch up to the little man. "Could you tell me exactly why we're going to this tower?"

"That depends," the Brownie said cagily. "Could you put your question in the form of a wish?"

"What?" Wuntvor exploded. "Must I use my wishes for everything?" His hand tightened around the hilt of his weapon. "If I weren't a hero and role model to unborn generations—"

"Careful now!" the sword cautioned him. "You know I don't like to be used for threats. It upsets my delicate balance."

The Brownie covered his head with his tiny hands, as if to ward off the lad's blows. "Hey!" he shouted as he continued up the hill backwards. "Don't blame me. You should see the wish quota I have to fill. Why do you think we're giving away seven wishes at a pop? For our health, maybe? It's tough being in the fairy tale—uh—*Brownie* tale business. If you're not on top of it all the time, your limelight gets stolen by a golden goose or something!"

"Indeed," Wuntvor replied, feeling his grasp of the situation once again slipping away, "perhaps we should continue to the tower."

"That's more like it!" the Brownie cheered enthusiastically. "I don't suppose you'd want to rephrase that as a wish, either? Just asking! Let's get to that tower."

The Brownie turned and ran up the last third of the hill. Wuntvor was hard put to keep up with him.

"One maiden coming up!" the Brownie announced.

Wuntvor was too busy catching his breath to think of an

appropriate answer. The rumbling was much louder up here.
He could definitely feel it through the soles of his boots. The
lad wondered if he wanted to meet a maiden who caused rumbling like that. Still, he had left his native land in search of
adventure, and he supposed this qualified as that sort of thing.

"Ready?" the Brownie prompted.

Wuntvor took a deep breath and nodded.

"You got it," the wee fellow replied. "Now all you have to
say is 'Fair maiden, fair maiden, let down your hair!' "

"Fair maiden?" Wuntvor said tentatively.

"It's part of the second wish!" the Brownie insisted. "Say it!"

"Very well." Wuntvor looked up at the tower and did just that.
"Fair maiden, fair maiden, let down your hair!"

He heard a woman's voice call down above the rumbling:
"So you may climb my golden stair!"

Golden stair? Wuntvor frowned. What did that mean?

Something plummeted from the window above. Something
golden and shining. It was heading right for him!

Then everything went black.

FIVE

A wizard needs to be many things beyond a mere magician. Among the skills a student mage must cultivate is play-acting, a talent which may be more important than it might seem at first glance. "Why acting?" the novice wizard might ask, but the benefits will soon become apparent when that same mage must "act up a storm" for a spell that is not quite going as planned. And as to "playing," well, it is only after such a spell has gone horribly wrong, bringing destruction and great financial reversals upon your clients, that you realize how useful "playing dead" can be.

—*The Teachings of Ebenezum,*
VOLUME XXII

"There you are."

Wuntvor groaned, blinking in the bright light.

The Brownie smiled apologetically. "I suppose I should have warned you about the hair. When it grows as long as all that, it gets pretty hefty. Here. I've swept enough of it aside so that you can crawl free." He waved for Wuntvor to follow him.

The lad crawled through the opening, then stood and turned to see what had befallen him. He whistled softly. The Brownie was correct. There was more hair here than he had ever seen in one place before. The entire side of the tower was covered with it; cascading golden blond strands that reached all the way to the window high above. And the hair was so long that it gathered in great masses upon the ground, forming valleys and tiny hillocks all its own, so that it looked like some miniature and yet strangely hirsute landscape spread out before him.

"Well," the woman's voice called to him. "Are you going to climb up or not?"

"Oh, most assuredly he shall!" the Brownie shouted. The little fellow nudged Wuntvor's ankle. "Well, you want your damsel, don't you?"

Wuntvor nodded, a touch troubled by these proceedings. Shouldn't there be some way to meet a fair maiden without having to climb up her hair? Still, in a way he supposed it was his fault. He knew from his childhood reading that whenever you got involved in wish stories you had to be incredibly specific, or this sort of thing always happened.

He stepped forward and gathered enough hair in his hands to make a thick rope. He gripped the strands as best he could and hoisted himself aloft.

"Ouch!" came a cry from far overhead.

Wuntvor looked down doubtfully at the Brownie.

"Hey," the little fellow shrugged. "You want your maiden, you've got to do what she asks. That's the way this wish stuff works. No pain, no gain."

Wuntvor grabbed a hank of hair above him and pulled himself up again.

"Ooooh!" This time, the noise from the window was more of a moan than a sharp cry.

Wuntvor looked up to the window far overhead. "Are you sure you want me to do this?"

And the melodious voice called down:

"Would you just hurry and get up here before you pull out *all* my hair?"

Well, Wuntvor thought, one should never argue with a fair maiden. If climbing was what she desired, Wuntvor would ascend.

"Yow!" the cry came from the tower, and "Oof! Eeee! Erk! Yorp!" and other exclamations of a similar stripe, every time Wuntvor pulled himself farther up the rope of hair. The lad redoubled his efforts, for he wished to put an end to the maiden's suffering as soon as possible.

At last his hand grasped the stone window sill. He grabbed the sill with his other hand as well, and hoisted himself up so that he could throw his leg across the ledge.

"Well," the maiden remarked upon seeing him. " 'Tis about time." She wrinkled her brow and rubbed her head. "Next time, I may choose to be rescued by a lighter hero."

Wuntvor began to stammer an apology.

"Oh, nevermind," the damsel replied. " 'Twas not your fault, after all. I was the one who asked you here. Now, if you would give me a hand, we need to haul up my hair."

So Wuntvor helped the maiden to gather her hair from the tower wall and return it to her sitting room. As they were involved in this procedure, which was quite time consuming, the lad thought to make polite conversation. Thus he commented upon the length and lustre of her hair, and wondered how she kept it so.

"You don't know the half of it!" The damsel, who was quite attractive when she had her hair pushed away from her face, rolled her eyes heavenward. "Nobody ever told me having long hair would be like this. Brushing it a hundred strokes takes all day! And when it gets snarled"—she laughed ruefully—"it's murder!"

Suddenly, the rumbling began again, deep within the tower, so loud that Wuntvor had to cover his ears for a moment until it passed.

"What was that?" he asked with some trepidation.

"Oh, nothing." The fair damsel shrugged. "Only the dragon."

A dragon? The Brownie had never said there was going to be a dragon!

Wuntvor walked back to the window and scowled down at the little fellow.

"You'd better get up here!" the lad warned.

"Is that a wish?" the Brownie hollered.

Wuntvor wanted to scream. He could see it happening; one way or another, the Brownie would make him squander all his wishes. But perhaps there was another way. Maybe Wuntvor could help the maiden escape without ever having to confront the dragon.

"Wait there!" he called to the Brownie, then turned about and walked back to the sitting room, where the fair damsel was trying to find enough nooks and crannies in which to stuff her tremendous locks so that she might have room to breathe. Before he did any rescuing, the lad decided, he should ask the maiden's opinion on the matter. He briefly outlined what he considered the options to be, then asked what she desired most.

"What do I want most?" the damsel replied, fluttering her long and copious lashes. "I want to sing!"

"Sing?" the lad repeated, somewhat surprised.

The damsel nodded, cheerful at last. "When you've been trapped in a tower as long as I have, you can't imagine how much you long to do a musical number for an audience. Even an audience of one." She flashed her lovely smile. "It was so nice of you to ask me. I'll do a little ditty that's always been one of my favorites."

She cleared her throat, and, to the lad's astonishment, began to belt out a song:

> "Am I afraid of dungeon towers?
> Oh no, not little me.
> My locks can unlock any door;
> My curls will set me free."

She grabbed a mass of hair and stared at it, enraptured, as she sang again:

> "Men can come and go;
> I really couldn't care.
> But I'm in love,
> I'm so fond of,
> My glorious, glorious hair."

The damsel curtsied, apparently finished with her performance. The rumbling returned, somehow more rhythmic than before.

"Oh, thank you, Hubert!" the maiden called. "Thank you

all so very much." She smiled at Wuntvor again. "It's gratify-
ing to work with a dragon that appreciates my talents."

Wuntvor realized then what the heavy pounding that filled
the tower really was. It was applause—dragon applause. The
lad had some trouble comprehending exactly what this meant.
He decided to take a direct approach.

"But you are held a captive in this tower!" he said to the
maiden. "Don't you want to escape?"

The maiden bit her lovely lip. "Oh, I suppose so," she said
after a moment's pause. "But the dragon would have to come
along as well."

If the lad had been puzzled before, now he was totally confused. This made no sense whatsoever. Dragons were meant
to rumble, and threaten, and possibly devour, but never ever
to applaud. And as to escaping and taking the dragon along—
what had the Brownie gotten him into? Next time he saw the
little fellow, they would have words.

In the meantime, though, he would have to hurry to stay
with the maiden, who was leaving the sitting room by the
second door, which led into the tower's interior. Wuntvor
sprinted just behind, careful to stay ahead of the massive curls
that swirled along the floor beside him.

"We go down these stairs," the maiden said. They were in
the end of a short corridor. "Hubert waits below." She began
her descent.

The lad followed once again, realizing that he would have
to completely rethink his opinions on the relationship between
damsels and dragons. Unless, perhaps, there was some more
sinister motivation behind the damsel's actions; that, perhaps,
she was adept at luring her young suitors to their doom, say,
as a dragon's lunch? But no, Wuntvor dismissed that idea
almost as soon as it occurred to him. No one as sweet and
lovely as the maiden before him could be involved in such
treachery. But then another, even less pleasant thought struck
him with the force of a winter storm.

"Does the dragon do musical numbers as well?" he asked,
trepidation once again in his voice.

"Well," the maiden admitted, "he used to, but there are a
few difficulties with his present contract." She shook her head
sadly. "If he uses his voice in an improper fashion, there could

be dire consequences. But you didn't come here to hear our problems. It's time to talk to Hubert."

She continued down the stairs. The lad could think of nothing to do but follow. The worn stone steps seemed to wind about the inside of the tower wall. As they descended, the ceiling and inner wall grew farther and farther away until, in the dim illumination, Wuntvor could imagine that there were no other walls at all besides the one he ran his hand against for support.

"Hubert!" the maiden called. "Oh, Hubert!"

With that, the rumbling started anew, much louder than before. They were approaching light—wild, flickering light, like that of a dozen torches.

But the flame was not born of wooden torches. It came instead, in great fiery gouts, from a dragon's snout, which appeared less than a dozen paces away from the startled Wuntvor.

"Yowp!" the lad cried, but the dragon regarded him in silence.

"There you are!" The damsel clapped her hands in glee. "Hubert always was one to make a dramatic entrance. Especially now that he is no longer speaking."

The dragon rumbled and nodded its head, upon which, Wuntvor noted, the reptile wore a purple top hat.

"Being prevented from talking might be a great burden to anyone whose chosen career is the theater," the damsel continued. "Many an actor could let this turn of events drag him into a despair from which he might not recover. But not our Hubert." She pointed proudly at the giant lizard. "This dazzling dragon has turned Mother Duck's edict into a whole new career direction. Yes, no longer is Hubert a dragon actor. Now, instead, Hubert has become the world's first dragon mime!" She clapped her hands smartly. "What a trouper! Come on, Hubert! Show him your stuff!"

The huge reptile leaned forward, pushing his forepaws against some imaginary wall, while its rear feet seemed to be walking without getting anywhere. Wuntvor frowned. What was this supposed to mean?

"That's right!" the damsel exclaimed proudly. "It's a dragon walking against the wind! What genius!" She turned and looked to the lad for approval.

"Indeed," the lad remarked for want of anything else to say. "But weren't we escaping?"

"Yes, yes, you're right of course. Out there, beyond this tower is a world full of audiences waiting to applaud Hubert's talent. But look!" The damsel pointed once again at the reptile. "Hubert's doing a dragon washing windows! What style! What panache!"

"Indeed," Wuntvor commented again, trying not to get too distracted by the circular motions Hubert was making with his feet. With all this dragon business, the lad was thinking twice about becoming involved with this maiden happily ever after. He wondered if the Brownie would let him re-use a wish. He tapped the damsel on the shoulder, causing her to pause in her gushing praise.

"You wouldn't happen to know where the door is?" he asked.

"Certainly." The damsel beamed. "Just beyond Hubert there."

"Indeed," the lad responded. "What say we go through it?"

The damsel laughed. "And let the world know our little secret?" She skipped merrily toward the dragon, holding her hair back so that it would not trip her. "Oh Hubert, Hubert, we're going on tour!"

The dragon nodded and used its tail to push open the tower door, a door larger than any Wuntvor had ever seen—large enough at least to let a dragon through. With such an easy way out, Wuntvor wondered absently why the damsel and the dragon hadn't left before this. He supposed there had to be some reason, but before he could think of a way to ask about it, the air was again full of rumbling.

He turned to the damsel. "Is Hubert clearing his throat?"

The maiden shook her head. "Oh, dear, no, that isn't the dragon rumbling at all. Listen carefully. That noise has no tone whatsoever, no sense of dynamics. It's obviously totally un-trained. Besides, I think it's coming from underground."

Underground? Why was there something about that fact that made the lad uneasy?

"Once upon a time," Wuntvor whispered. "Once upon a time."

The rumbling grew louder, and a great rift appeared in the floor before them. The air became filled with dust, and when the dust cleared, Wuntvor saw that a long table had appeared from the hole in the earth. Seated behind that table were five of the ugliest creatures he had ever seen.

The creature in the center pounded a gavel.

"We claim this land in the name of the Netherhells!"

A gavel? The Netherhells? Thoughts and images raced madly about in the lad's brain.

"Indeed," he managed weakly.

"Wuntie?" the damsel cried in alarm. "Is something wrong?"

The lad managed a choked laugh. "Oh, nothing much. I just wish I knew what was going on here!"

"Granted!" a tiny voice screamed at his side.

SIX

Memory is a funny thing. I can't begin to tell you how many times I have forgotten to keep an appointment with the royal tax collector. This always seems to upset the official greatly, until I mention that perhaps I can make up for my error and help facilitate their inspection of my gold by transforming the official into a sparrow, so that he might fly there directly, or into a frog, so that he might hop quickly from one source of wealth to the next, or—perhaps best of all—into a worm, so that he might burrow beneath the earth searching for hidden assets. Oddly enough, every time we have this conversation, the tax collector forgets to make any further appointments. As I said, memory is a funny thing.

—*Wizardnetics: Your Guide
to Total Magical Fulfillment,*
by Ebenezum, Greatest Wizard
in the Western Kingdom
(thirty-fourth edition)

That did it. Everything came rushing back at once. It was like

getting hit in the face with Hendrek's warclub. I remembered
Mother Duck and my quest and companions, and the attacks
of the Netherhells and the plight of Vushta and my master and
my current situation with Norei and any number of other things.

"Um—," I remarked. "Indeed." I remembered again that I
had to somehow convince Mother Duck of the error of her
ways. But could I do that while we were being attacked by the
Netherhells?

"Wait a second!" the small demon at the end of the table
exclaimed in a grating voice. "This isn't Vushta!"

The large demon at table's center pounded its gavel. "What
do you mean? You remember our discussions. The remaining
magical might of the surface world has concentrated itself in
Vushta. You yourself recall the hundred or more wizards we
faced last time we were there." The demon waved its gavel at
the clearing around the table. "Well, this was where all the
magic was emanating from. And we followed that magic to
get here. Therefore, this must be Vushta."

"Point of order!" the small demon objected. "This doesn't
look at all like Vushta."

The main demon waved its gavel even more furiously, as if
to disperse the other's objection into the late summer air. "So
they've disguised it. Whenever you're facing more than a
hundred magicians, you have to expect clever things like that."

"No, no, no, no, no!" Mother Duck's voice grew in intensity
as she rushed down the hill toward us. "It's all wrong! Why
does this sort of thing have to happen to me?"

"Perhaps," Jeffrey called as he attempted to catch up to her,
"things would go better if you would employ a few talking
wolves. Improvisation is a skill much prized among wolfkind—"

"Hey!" a voice called, close by my foot. "Are you just going
to let me lay here and rust?"

I looked down. It was Cuthbert, my magic sword. I realized
I must have dropped it when the hair had fallen on me.

I knelt and picked the weapon up.

"Much better!" Cuthbert crowed. "The first thing the hero
must learn is the proper care of his weapons. And when his
weapon is something as magical as mmmmpphh!"

I rapidly slid Cuthbert back into its scabbard. I had other

things to think about besides lessons in proper sword care. I wondered how I might get Mother Duck's attention, but from the way she was glaring at the demonic newcomers, I had a feeling that reasoned discussion was one of the furthest things from her mind.

One of the other demons pointed at the rapidly approaching woman. "I think we may be under attack."

"Is it time to boil blood?" the end demon asked enthusiastically.

Mother Duck shook both her fists as she barreled toward the committee.

"Oh dear," the gavel demon remarked, a slight quaver in its voice. "Perhaps we are not in Vushta after all."

"What are you doing here?" Mother Duck demanded as she rushed before the demons. "I certainly hope you're not here on one of your missions of conquest!"

"Oh! No, no! Never conquest!" the gavel demon insisted. It paused, cowering ever so slightly. When it became apparent that Mother Duck was not going to smite the creature where it stood, the demon wiped its brow and continued in a more moderate tone: "Well, actually, we were on one of our missions, but not to the Eastern Kingdoms—never to the Eastern Kingdoms, I assure you. We simply got a little turned around. . . ." The demon's voice died under Mother Duck's withering stare.

"Anyone could have made that mistake," another of the demons added.

"You see," explained the small, sickly fellow down at the end, "it's dark underground, and the signage isn't all that good either."

"Am I expected to believe—," Mother Duck began slowly.

"No, of course not!" the sickly demon agreed. "We'd never expect you to believe that!"

"There could be another reason why we're here," the gavel demon chimed in, speaking even more rapidly than before. "Say—we missed you. Of course. That's it. Certainly." The demon tugged at its too tight collar. "Uh—you don't know what a trial it's been not to see your face. Right. It's been—well, *hours* since our last encounter, and we were so looking forward to your inspirational—"

"Silence!" Mother Duck commanded.

The demons silenced.

In the sudden absence of noise, I heard other rustlings behind me. I glanced around to see Snarks, Brax and Guxx climbing up the riverbank.

"And don't you try anything, either!" Mother Duck proclaimed, fixing the three with her steely glare. She turned back to the committee. "You remember what happened the last time you tried to boil blood around here?"

All five demons nodded their heads vigorously.

"Certainly, Mother Duck."

"Most assuredly, Mother Duck."

"The survivors are still under the care of the finest physicians in the Netherhells, Mother Duck."

"Very well," the woman stated. "We won't have any more of that sort of thing, will we?"

The five demons blanched noticeably, turning pastel shades of their various fantastic hues.

"Oh, no, Mother Duck."

"Absolutely not, Mother Duck."

"You have it all there in writing, Mother Duck. Would you like us to recite it aloud?"

But before Mother Duck could respond, another gruff demonic voice interjected:

"Begin!"

Brax beat on the drum he had thoughtfully slung from his waist.

> "Guxx Unfufadoo, appalled demon,
>   Has had his fill of Netherhells' cowards;
>   Will grab them by soft underbellies,
>   And feed them to the molten slime pits!"

Guxx flexed his claws as if they could barely wait for the aforementioned grabbing and feeding to begin.

The committee all stared at their former leader, he who had once been Grand Hoohah. Mother Duck was temporarily forgotten. Guxx's pronouncement had clearly upset them.

"Oh, yeah?" exploded the small, sickly fiend at table's end.

"You and what army?" the fellow next to him rejoined.

"Why don't you come over *here* and say that?" something shouted from the other end of the table.

The primary demon pounded its gavel.

"Now, then," it rumbled grimly at Guxx. "Let us get something clear. You were once a power in the Netherhells, but you are a power no more. We now hold the reins of the world below. If you choose to question our might, there will be"—the fiend paused for dramatic effect—"retribution."

"Oh, yeah!" the small, sickly fellow exclaimed enthusiastically.

Mother Duck stepped between the combatants.

"I think not," she said calmly, staring at the five demon committee members. "You will do nothing of the kind. Those already here are under my protection."

I could not believe my ears. Mother Duck, our sworn enemy, was actually defending us! I wondered for an instant what had caused her change of heart, and decided it had to be our obvious sincerity. As we participated in her fairy stories, she was coming to know our true, honest selves. Perhaps it wouldn't be so difficult to reason with her after all!

"But these are demons!" the gavel fiend persisted. "They are ours by Netherhells' common law!"

"Oh, boy! Is it time to boil blood?" The sickly fellow grinned at my three demonic allies as its fellow committee members also turned their collective gaze in the same direction. "Feeling a little hot under the collars, boys?"

Snarks and Brax both quietly retreated behind the greater bulk of Guxx Unfufadoo.

Mother Duck reached a hand inside her woolen vest. She pulled out a sheaf of parchment. "You are perhaps forgetting this," she remarked casually. "This is the contract I signed with the Netherhells after our last unfortunate incident, a contract which supercedes all Netherhells laws, prevents all demonic interference in my kingdoms and is possibly the only reason why the Netherhells still exist!"

"That's telling them!" Snarks cheered, poking his head out to the left of Guxx.

"One should always abide by contracts," Brax added as he peeked out from the right.

I tried hard to repress a smile. Mother Duck seemed definitely to be swinging to our side in this discussion. As soon as this little altercation was over, I resolved to speak with the woman, addressing her as the ally I was sure she would become. I stared at the ground, searching for the exact words. How would my master handle this?

"We certainly don't object," the gavel demon interjected hastily. "We would never object with Mother Duck!" The other committee demons nodded their agreement.

Mother Duck smiled. "I'm glad everyone sees things my way. There will be no more threats against these demons. You are interlopers." She gestured at the committee, then turned and waved in much the same fashion at the rest of us. "Those already here are pawns. They are mine to do with as I choose."

Pawns? Do with as she chose? That wasn't the way one spoke about potential allies. I frowned. Perhaps I had slightly misinterpreted recent events. Maybe I should address Mother Duck as more of a neutral party.

"Consider yourself lucky, demons," the old woman continued. "This time, I will accept your pitiful excuses, and look upon your visit here as an oversight. But listen closely: if I see you again, the Netherhells will pay!"

The demons all began to talk at once:

"Certainly, Mother Duck."

"Our every effort is to please you, Mother Duck."

"We will do whatever you ask, Mother Duck," the gavel demon added. "We ask only one boon. Might you, in your infinite wisdom, be able to point out the way to Vushta and the Western Kingdoms?"

Mother Duck sighed. "Very well, even though it isn't in the contract. I can see no other way to be rid of you for good." She pointed over the demon's shoulder. "That way."

The demon twisted its head around, still perplexed. "That's all you can tell me? That way? You couldn't be a little more specific?"

The other demons nudged their leader.

"That's perfectly all right, Mother Duck," one bubbled.

"Thank you for all the help, Mother Duck," another chirped.

"Don't you think it's time we were going so that we can leave Mother Duck and her pawns in peace?" the sickly fiend asked hopefully.

"Remember the contract!" Mother Duck whispered helpfully.

"The contract?" The gavel demon repressed a shiver. "Very well, Mother Duck. I never meant to question your directions, Mother Duck. Uh—that way." It nodded toward the west. "Back into the earth, fellow demons!"

Grunting and groaning, the committee dragged their table back to the edge of the crevice, and then, with a final heave-ho, toppled it into the pit. The five demons quickly followed.

"At last!" Mother Duck glanced about at the rest of us, clapping her hands peremptorily. "No dawdling, now. Back to work!"

"But—," I began. She didn't even seem to hear me as she marched back toward the hill, the talking wolf in close pursuit. How could I convince her of the wisdom of our cause if she wouldn't even stop and listen?

"Oh, Wuntie!" Alea breathed in my ear. "She called us pawns!"

"Indeed," I replied, wishing that the damsel would not stand quite so close. "I believe she underestimates us. She is so wrapped up in concocting her fairy stories that she ignores us when we are not under her direct control. We must therefore use this time wisely, and complete our escape plans."

The former Grand Hoohah stepped forward, raising both his clawed hands to gain our attention.

"Commence!" Guxx intoned.

I placed a restraining hand on Guxx's shoulder. "Please, no declaiming—" I glanced at Hubert and Alea. "—or singing for that matter—until I'm finished. I fear our time is limited."

"It's even shorter than that!" Snarks remarked. "The old lady's already made it to the top of the hill."

"No, not quite yet," Hubert said, motioning the truth-telling demon to silence. "She's still talking to the wolf. Something about how having hirsute characters in your stories gives those tales a gritty realism. We have a moment yet." The dragon grinned. "Always depend on dragon ears."

Snarks nodded. "I'd rather do that than listen to a dragon's vocal chords."

"Indeed," I interjected. "I fear there is no time for an argument, either. But Snarks's remark about vocal chords reminds me of the way Mother Duck controls us. Each of us falls under her spell through the use of our own voices. I believe we could actually break free of her spell, if only there was some way we could keep from saying those words. All of us must concentrate—"

"Those words?" Guxx rumbled.

"You mean 'Once upon a time'?" Hubert added helpfully.

Something strange happened to the dragon as soon as he framed the question. The huge reptile's eyes glazed over, and he began to totter back and forth.

"Look out!" Alea cried.

The rest of the party rapidly retreated as Hubert finally tottered too far and fell upon his back. When the dust settled, I saw that he was grabbing great handfuls of air with his forepaws while his legs kicked out against an invisible barrier.

"What is Hubert doing?" I asked, already afraid of the answer.

"Can't you tell?" Alea replied, excited despite herself. "It's a dragon doing the backstroke! He's back in the fairy story. But what talent!"

So saying the four words turned Hubert instantly back into a dragon mime. I nodded grimly. "This proves my point. If we can only resist, we may be able to overcome this spell!"

"But how can we resist?" Tap asked urgently. "Her spells are even stronger than Brownie Power!"

"We simply must be very careful about what we say, and never put those four words together in a sentence. Now concentrate with me, so that we might prevail."

I took a deep breath. I had broken into a sudden sweat. Was Mother Duck already attempting to exert her magical control over me? I waved for the others to come closer. "Now listen to me," I began. "*Once* Mother Duck gets us under her control, we are lost, for who knows *upon* what whim she will once again relinquish her control." My head was beginning to swim. I bit my lip, willing the pain to clear my mind. "Now, all we have to do is take her spells one at *a time*—"

I blinked. Something had changed. What was I saying? What had I said? Why was everyone around me saying the same thing?

Had something gone wrong with one of my wishes?

SEVEN

I admit it. I have always had a weakness for damsels with long blond hair. Well, actually, I have a bit of a weakness for brunette maidens as well. Ah, yes—and then there are damsels with hair of fire red! And did you ever notice how attractive women can be when they are totally bald?

—An uncompleted later chapter of
Some Thoughts About Apprenticeship,
by Wuntvor, apprentice to Ebenezum,
greatest wizard in the Western Kingdoms
(a work in progress)

Once upon a time, Wuntvor had thought this whole wish thing with the Brownie might bring him his fortune. Now he wasn't so sure.

"Now where were we?" the Brownie asked helpfully. "Oh, yes, you had just escaped from the tower with the maiden and the dragon, and having used three wishes, were wondering what next to do on your quest for adventure."

Wuntvor frowned. The Brownie's summation sounded fun-

57

damentally correct, and certainly went a long way toward calming the confusion that rattled about in his skull. There was only one thing that troubled him.

"Three wishes?" he queried.

The Brownie nodded his tiny head.

Wuntvor shook his in turn, still trying to remember. "I had wished for . . . a weapon. Oh, yes! And to find a woman to be my love. What was my third wish?"

"That you wanted to know everything!" the Brownie replied.

Wuntvor scratched his head. "Then why don't I remember it?"

The Brownie looked at Wuntvor solemnly, then glanced at the hill beyond. "Believe me, you don't want to know."

What? Wuntvor now found himself so confused that he couldn't even frame another question. He was beginning to suspect, however, that this whole conversation was a Brownie trick to get him to waste another wish. Perhaps it would be best to go on to other matters.

"Oh, Wuntie!" the beautiful maiden called to him. How did she know his name? Had they ever officially been introduced? "We have great news for you!"

"Once upon a time," Wuntvor murmured as he turned to face the long-haired beauty, for those words somehow seemed to calm him. "Once upon a time."

"Hubert and I have been thinking," the damsel continued. "It is difficult for an unattached man and woman to travel through the countryside. There are malicious gossips everywhere, and certain people who will always think the worst. Of course, having a dragon along does help somewhat. For some reason, people are reticent to speak their worst excesses in the vicinity of a fire-breathing reptile. Still, we might have trouble if your presence is not properly explained. Therefore—"

She paused while the dragon leapt about from foot to foot in what could charitably be called a dance. The giant lizard waved its top hat in Wuntvor's direction.

"Can't you see what Hubert's trying to tell you?" The damsel cheered. "You're going to become part of our act!"

"Indeed," the lad replied, somewhat startled by this information. Somehow, becoming part of a touring company with a beautiful damsel and dancing dragon was not his precise definition of "adventure." Still, he was willing to attempt anything, as long as a lovely maiden was about. Besides which, he reflected, it was easy to make decisions of this type if you still had four Brownie wishes to fall back on.

"Indeed," he said again.

The damsel clapped her hands happily. "Oh, we'll have such fun! And listen, we even have an idea for our first routine. It's an old one, but that means it's a proven audience pleaser."

The dragon blew an elaborate smoke ring by way of agreement.

"That's right," the maiden trilled. "I'm talking about the Thrilling Dragon Rescue!" She glanced up at the large reptile apologetically. "I know that's species stereotyping, but what are you going to do? It's what they expect out in the sticks. And we are definitely in the sticks." She smiled at Wuntvor. She was lovely when she smiled. "Are you ready?"

The lad nodded his head somewhat dubiously.

"Right, here we go," the damsel replied. "First, Hubert will breathe a little fire to set the mood."

The dragon roared above them, flame shooting the length of the clearing.

"Now," the damsel instructed, "it is time for you to stare bravely at Hubert and draw your sword."

Wuntvor did as he was told.

"What's going on here?" the sword demanded, its voice cracking in its haste.

The damsel assured the weapon that it was only needed for a demonstration.

"Oh, really? You're sure about that?" the sword replied, somewhat mollified. "You'll have to excuse me, but in my line of work, it's easy to get jumpy. I mean, here you are, sitting snug in the dark, lulled into complacency by the steady slap-slap-slap of scabbard against thigh, then whizzo, you're out in the sunlight. Wouldn't you find that the slightest bit disconcerting?"

"I had never thought of it from a sword's point of view," the damsel mused. "Still, now that you are in the theater, we should be able to avoid that problem entirely. In our act, you will know exactly when you will be drawn, and precisely what you are supposed to do."

She turned back to me. "Now, Wuntie, point the sword away from you at arm's length, and run straight for the dragon's breastbone."

"Wait a minute!" Cuthbert wailed, the panic back in its voice. "This is just another trick to get me into battle, isn't it?" The sword laughed ruefully. "I know the way it is around here. I mean, I remember what my old uncle used to tell me—he was an enchanted brass headboard, and knew all about these things—he'd say, 'Cuthbert, my boy, never get involved with heroes. Heroes are always hacking or slashing something. Stay away from practical swords and daggers. Go for ornamental, my boy,' he said. But did I listen? Oh, no! Magic latticework was too dull for me! Magic locks and keys didn't get to go places and do things! So I end up becoming a talking sword; nothing but a hero's *tool!* "

"Now, now," the lad reassured the overwrought blade in his hand. "I've always had great respect for my weapons. And I will only draw you when it is time for action."

"I know it," the sword replied bitterly. "Then you'll *use* me! Oh, the trials of being an intelligent inanimate object!"

"Indeed," Wuntvor answered solemnly, wishing to put an end to these histrionics. "Cuthbert, we are acting out a play. There will be no cutting, and no blood."

"No cutting?" the sword quavered.

"Indeed," the lad replied.

"No blood?" Cuthbert asked.

"No blood," Alea reassured the weapon.

"Well, why didn't you say so?" Cuthbert cleared its throat. "Go forth, brave warrior! Your noble sword will lead the way!"

"I'm glad we've got that out of the way," the maiden said. "Motivation is so often a problem in our line of work. Now, Wuntie! Thrust your sword forth and rush the marauding beast!"

"Should I say anything?" the lad asked.

"An excellent idea," the damsel agreed. "A bloodcurdling epithet or two would be perfectly in character."

"Indeed," the lad replied, taking a deep breath before he began his run.

He shouted as he picked up speed, hoping to find an appropriate phrase: "I'll get you—uh—beast—uh—reptile—uh—uh—you'd better watch out uh—I've got a sword here."

"Well, we'll have to work on your epithets," the maiden said as she stepped in front of the dragon. The lad skidded to a halt, his shining sword mere inches from the maiden's massive hair. The damsel smiled. "You are, however, very good at stopping. As you see, the brave hero is brought up short by the appearance of the beauteous maiden. However, the hero does not truly fall in love with the maiden until she begins her song."

A song? Hadn't something like this happened to Wuntvor before? Oh, yes, up in the tower. But he had the feeling that it had occurred many other times as well. The young man looked around. Where was the Brownie when he needed him?

But it was too late. The damsel had already begun to sing:

"If you've got a dragon,
 You'll never be cold;
 But he will eat you
 Before you get old!

"If you've got a dragon,
 You'll never get wet,
 Unless all that fire
 Works up a sweat!

"If you've got a dragon,
 I've got a hunch,
 Your future is short,
 And it's probably lunch!

"Take me from this dragon,
 Oh please set me free;
 Or I will be flame-broiled
 On its rotisserie!

"Now you'll be a hero,
 Please don't be a slob!
 Or soon I will end up
 A damsel-kebab!"

The song ran on, verse after verse. After a time, Wuntvor

decided to sit, resting his talking sword gently across his knees.

"We don't get much of a part in this, do we?" the sword remarked.

The lad nodded and sighed. "This acting stuff isn't all that I had hoped. It doesn't seem to be much more than a lot of waiting around." He glanced up at the damsel, who was singing a verse about dragon fritters. "I do wish this could be a little more exciting."

"Granted!" came a little voice from nowhere.

Wuntvor heard heavy footsteps crossing the bridge behind him. He stood, turning so quickly that he almost lost his sword.

A massive warrior stood on the near end of the bridge, holding a huge warclub in one of his very large hands.

"Doom," the warrior intoned. "The time of reckoning has come."

EIGHT

It is difficult for some people to realize that giants, like many other huge magical creatures, are largely misunderstood. Think on it, however. How many times are you going to have a reasoned, caring conversation with a creature from whom you are fleeing for your very life?

—*I'm OK, I'm a wizard: The Magician's Guide to Perfect Mental Health,* by Ebenezum, greatest mage in the Western Kingdoms (fourth edition)

"Let's not get any rash ideas," the sword cautioned.

"Shall we see what this warrior wants?" Wuntvor suggested.

Cuthbert groaned softly. "Oh, I knew this was going to be a bad day. You know what I mean? Did you ever have the feeling that you've gotten up out of the wrong side of the scabbard?"

"Doom," the large warrior rumbled as the lad approached. "Norei is waiting. I was supposed to say that."

Norei is waiting? Hope suddenly sprang in Wuntvor's breast. But that meant that—

"Once upon a time," the warrior and the lad said in unison.

63

"Doom," the large fellow repeated. "I am the warrior of warning. And I am warning you: The giant is coming."

"The giant?" Cuthbert and the damsel screamed in unison. Even the dragon took a few involuntary steps backward.

"The giant?" the lad replied. "I guess that's bad?"

"The giant can find you, no matter where you hide," the sword wailed.

"The giant knows no mercy!" Alea added.

"Doom!" the warrior of warning concluded.

"I guess it is bad," Wuntvor said. "What am I to do?"

"Hide!" the sword screamed. "All is lost! There is no hope!"

"I fear that your weapon is incorrect," the damsel stated boldly. "Where there is theater, there is always hope! But how best to use your newfound abilities?"

The dragon rumbled overhead. Both Wuntvor and the maiden looked up to see the reptile waving his forepaws in a slow rhythm. When the paws were spread apart, the lizard moved his head back and forth, as if it studied something.

"Of course!" the damsel cried as she applauded. "What genius. It is an honor, Hubert, to be working with you!"

"Indeed," Wuntvor interjected when there appeared to be no explanation forthcoming. "I am sure it is truly a subtle piece of genius. Would you mind giving me a hint as to its exact meaning?"

"Oh, can't you see?" Alea cheered. "It's a dragon mime reading a newspaper!"

A newspaper? Wuntvor frowned. That word was somehow familiar. Didn't that have something to do with a chicken crossing the road?

"Indeed," the lad said at last. "What's a newspaper?"

The damsel pulled a piece of parchment from her bodice. As she unfolded the sheet, Wuntvor saw it was covered with dense script.

"This is a newspaper!" she declared. "To be more specific, a trade newspaper!"

Wuntvor found this new statement no more illuminating than what had been said before. However, he was sure that, if he remained quiet, it would all be explained to him, at least after a fashion.

"I tell you, if you want to move around in this business, you simply have to keep up with the trades." The maiden rapidly scanned the page. "All we have to do is give you a new identity. The giant won't be able to find you if you no longer exist!"

"Indeed?" So that was their plan? Wuntvor was still not convinced.

"Ah!" the maiden called in triumph. "There's a town named Bremen that's looking for some musicians. Opportunities are everywhere!" She shook the parchment in the lad's direction. "See? Here's another place—Hamlin. 'Piper wanted.' All you need is a few simple flute tunes. . . ."

She frowned as she continued to read. "Well, I don't know about that one. Being a musical leader for a bunch of rats isn't everybody's idea of a good time. It always pays to read these things all the way through."

"Doom," the warrior interjected. "You have no time to read. The giant is coming."

The damsel ignored the sword's hysterical screams to stare critically at Wuntvor. "Perhaps we do not have time to give you a new identity, but theater will save you yet! It is time for a quick disguise."

"Indeed?" the lad asked. Well, he had asked for adventure, and now, apparently, he had it. He stuffed his sword back in its sheath so that all he heard was an occasional muffled whimper. Perhaps it was time then to come up with some disguise that would allow him to flee unhindered through the forest; a brave soldier, perhaps, on an unnamed mission from which he could not pause, or a simple woodsman, rushing home after a trying workday. The lad resolved that, whatever the charade, he would act it to make the maiden proud.

The damsel looked about quickly. "We have little enough at hand. We will have to use a length of my hair."

"We will?" the lad queried, somewhat surprised by this turn of events. Should a brave soldier have long, blond hair? Or would it be more appropriate to a humble woodsman?

"Alas, it is all that is available to me," the damsel replied. "Have no fear. I shan't miss it. You wouldn't believe how fast it grows. Hubert! I have need of your claws."

The dragon obligingly knelt nearby, shearing off a length of the maiden's locks with one reptilian forefinger.

The damsel picked up the newly freed mass of hair with a

smile. "Now all we need is a length of sackcloth that we can wrap like a skirt to hide your leggings. Hubert, if you could nip back into the tower larder to see what we have?"

The dragon nodded and nipped.

"Now." The beautiful maiden bit her perfectly formed lip as she surveyed Wuntvor's skull. "We will need my sash to serve as a headband to keep the hair in place."

"Indeed?" the lad remarked hesitantly. "If I may ask, what is this disguise to be?"

"You will masquerade as a fair maiden—" She frowned at his face. "Well, at least as a maiden, until you have left the vicinity. The hair is long enough to disguise you above the waist, and the skirt should hide your lower extremities as well. Once you are beyond the Eastern Kingdoms, you can remove the wig and resume your true identity."

"A maiden?" the lad began to protest. "But—"

"Doom," the warrior of warning interjected. "The giant."

"Indeed," Wuntvor replied. "The giant." He stood still while the real damsel adjusted the hair and headband, then wrapped about his waist a long piece of brown cloth that the dragon had brought.

"There," the beautiful maiden said at last. "You'll do. The hair will fall in your face, further masking your features. Just don't let anybody get too close to you."

"Indeed." At least the lad could agree with the last remark. "Now you must excuse me while I make my escape." The sooner he was shed of this silly disguise, the better.

"Doom," the warrior agreed. "Leave quickly."

"But take smaller steps," the damsel coached as Wuntvor moved away. "And hold your head up. Remember, you are a refined maiden now."

Wuntvor didn't respond. He felt more like a refined dustmop with all the hair in his face. And he almost tripped on the long skirt. How did people walk in these things, anyway?

Still, from the way the others had spoken of the giant, this appeared to be his only chance for survival. He had no choice but to ignore how ludicrous he looked and hope he could escape from this place before anything truly embarrassing happened.

"Farewell, Wuntie!" the damsel called as he began his flight in earnest. "Perhaps some day we can act together again, in more intimate surroundings!"

Wuntvor waved a final time, careful not to move his head too quickly, lest he dislodge the mass of hair. Even taking smaller steps, he was soon out of sight of the others, surrounded by the ancient Eastern forest.

"Well, hello there," a beautifully modulated voice spoke from the nearby underbrush. "I almost didn't recognize you."

Wuntvor stopped short. Could this be the giant? He reached for his sword.

But something considerably shorter than a giant stepped from between the bushes. Still, despite its smaller size, it was more wondrous than a giant could ever be.

"A—a unicorn," the lad said aloud.

"Not just any unicorn," the beast replied proudly. "The unicorn. Your unicorn. Could you have forgotten me so soon? Oh, of course you could. You're in one of her fairy tales, aren't you?"

"Once upon a time," the lad replied.

The creature sighed magnificently. "This might be more difficult than I thought. And after I've traveled so far to see you again. If not for that certain quality you have—" The unicorn looked at him meaningfully. "You know what I'm talking about. I can't help myself." The beast shuddered gloriously. "And now this."

"Do I know you from somewhere?" the lad replied, for he couldn't remember this beast at all, which was doubly disturbing, since the unicorn was one of the most memorable things he had ever seen.

"I know," the creature said with a profound sadness. "I've got eyes, don't I? I can see what you're doing: Practicing to join one of the forbidden delights as soon as I've gone. You know how desperately I need to rest my weary head! How can you toy with my affections so?" The beast brushed at the lad's blond wig with its lustrous golden horn. "It's even worse when you get kinky!"

"Indeed," the lad said, still uncertain of what the magnificent beast was going on about, but increasingly glad for his ignorance. "I'm sure what you are saying is all very interesting, and I would be glad to discuss it with you at some other time. Now, if you will excuse me, I have a forest to flee."

"Well, if you are in such a hurry," the unicorn remarked coyly, "I suppose I can't tell you about Norei."

"Norei?" Why did that name send a shiver down his spine? Why did the words "one true love" fill his brain? Of course!

"Once up—" Wuntvor clamped his lips tight before he could finish the phrase. This was no time for reassurance. There were serious things to consider. He thought of Norei again, and a young woman's face burned its way into his consciousness. The young witch. His only love. Norei. It took his breath away.

"Are you all right?" the unicorn inquired.

Wuntvor took a deep breath, remembering to stand up straight. "Indeed," he replied.

"That's a relief," the beast remarked. "It seemed you were having a spasm of some sort. I'd hate to lose you now, when we've gotten so close."

"But what of Norei?" Wuntvor asked, wishing to hear more of her. "Do you mind if we walk as we talk? I'm afraid I'm trying to escape."

The unicorn trotted wondrously alongside as Wuntvor began to walk swiftly but casually. Smaller steps, the young man reminded himself.

"Well, of course, Norei's the reason why I'm here." The creature wriggled its splendid eyebrows. "Well, at least that's *one* of the reasons."

"And Norei?" the lad prompted.

The unicorn sighed. "Well, if we must. Norei has a plan for your escape. Now remember these words: Happily ever after!"

"Happily ever after?" the lad repeated.

"Exactly. Said at the proper moment, those words will set you free. Mother Duck will hold sway over you no more."

"Mother Duck?" Wuntvor asked, suddenly remembering her as well. "But how did you escape her control?"

"It is in the nature of being a unicorn." The beast sniffed magnificently. "My coat is so white, my hooves so swift, my horn so blinding in the summer sun, that Mother Duck's spells reflect off me and can do me no harm."

"Indeed?" the lad said, wondering if this information might do him some good at a later time.

"Certainly," the wondrous creature murmured proudly. "Why do you think unicorns appear in so few fairy tales? Mother Duck can't use what she can't catch."

"So Norei—," Wuntvor began.

"Norei, Norei, always Norei!" the unicorn wailed. It paused, pointing its shining horn at the leaf-strewn ground. "No, it is quite all right. Forgive my outburst. I am myself again. What can my longing do but make me a better beast?" The creature looked at the lad with its deep and soulful eyes. "For what is perfect beauty without perfect pain?"

"And Norei?" the lad insisted.

"Yes, yes, of course," the unicorn added hastily. "She will save you, of course, if you simply remember the magic words. Of course. Still—"

The magic creature paused again, its eyes filled with the greatest sadness Wuntvor had ever seen.

"Is there something else you wish to say?" the lad asked.

"Well," the beast began hesitantly, "I was just thinking . . . my head is so heavy . . . and your lap is so near . . . so inviting . . ." The beast shivered wondrously. "I realize you are not entirely yourself and it wouldn't mean quite the same thing—well, a beast can dream, can't it?"

"Indeed," Wuntvor responded, wishing he could find a way to change the subject. "I'm sure we might be able to come to some arrangement, if I weren't in the midst of fleeing for my life—my, did you ever see such a large tree in your life?"

And, indeed, there was a huge tree before them, perhaps twenty times the circumference of any of its neighbors. Stranger still, this tree was not the usual deep brown of the others in the forest, but was closer to the green of meadow grass.

"That's no tree," the unicorn replied. "That's a beanstalk."

"A beanstalk?" the lad rolled the word around his tongue. "Indeed. And what is a beanstalk?"

The unicorn looked at the lad incredulously. "Surely you know what big beanstalks are for. They take you up to where the giants live."

"Once upon a time!" the lad cried in surprise. For, when he looked up the beanstalk, he saw someone descending from far overhead.

An incredibly deep voice wafted down from the clouds.

"Oops!" the voice said.

NINE

They tell you to "always watch your feet." But if you're constantly looking at your feet, how can you tell where you're going?

—*Some Notes on Apprenticeship,*
by Wuntvor, apprentice to Ebenezum,
greatest mage in the Western Kingdoms
(a work in progress)

Something was falling very rapidly from the sky. Something that Wuntvor suspected would be much heavier on impact than a mass of hair.

"I suggest that we move as quickly as possible back into the forest," the unicorn called, already on the move.

"I think I need to do more than that!" Wuntvor exclaimed. "That's the giant I've been trying to get away from."

The unicorn risked a final look aloft. "Well, I fear that this particular giant is going to be very close very soon."

"Indeed!" the lad yelled back, redoubling his speed. "I just wish I had some place to hide."

"Granted!" a small but very chipper voice yelled nearby.

Wuntvor screamed as a pit opened up beneath him.

*   *   *

The lad opened his eyes. He couldn't see a thing. With some trepidation, he parted the mass of hair that had descended in front of his face. He looked at an expanse of light gray rock. He lifted his gaze and saw that he had fallen into a cave of some sort, but it was a well-lit cave, swept and tidy besides, obviously the sort of place someone or something called home.

Wuntvor peered carefully through his disguise. As far as he could tell, there was no one moving about. But didn't he smell food?

Until this instant, the lad had not realized how hungry he was. When was the last time he had eaten? Wuntvor couldn't remember, but then there were so many things he could not recall.

"Once upon a time," the lad murmured as he walked toward the warm food smells. He turned a corner in the cave, and found that the home that he had stumbled upon was not simply a resting place for some creature from the wild. No, there were furnishings here; places to sit and hangings upon the wall, although none of it was quite like anything he had ever seen.

Wuntvor warily circled a trio of stools. They looked much like ordinary stools except that each had a seat covered with some sort of cloth padding. Well, he didn't imagine that padding could hurt him, so perhaps he should try sitting down, especially since the warm food smells came from the table just beyond.

The lad sat first in the tallest stool. But he leapt off in an instant, barely stifling a cry of pain. His posterior stung in half a dozen places. That stool hadn't been soft at all. Rather, the padding seemed to be filled with sharpened rocks. Wuntvor had never felt anything so hard in his life.

The lad tentatively felt the padding on the second stool, wary of further tricks. But this cloth was what he expected, soft and pliable. Perhaps the first stool was a trick of some sort, placed there for unwary visitors. Then again, it could have been built for something that enjoyed sitting on sharpened rocks. Wuntvor fervently hoped for the first alternative.

Still, there were three large pieces of pie on the table beyond the stools, and their aroma was making Wuntvor's taste buds scream for sustenance. The lad decided he would have to try the second chair after all. He climbed the stool and sat gingerly.

Ah, that was much better, Wuntvor thought as he sank into the padding. But shouldn't he stop sinking? There seemed to be no seat under the stuffing. The lad felt he would sink forever. He leapt from the stool as best he could. He never realized anything could be that soft!

Wuntvor stood there for a long moment, waiting for his heart to quiet down. Perhaps he should leave this place before he got into further trouble. If only he weren't so hungry!

Well, there was always the third stool. It was the smallest of the three, so he would be able to easily get away should there be any trouble. And, now that the lad thought about it, neither of the first two stools had caused him any serious damage.

Well, he was here to go on adventures, the lad reasoned, and, considering what had happened thus far, sitting on the small stool qualified. He took a deep breath and sat.

To his surprise, the stool felt wonderfully comfortable. It was like sitting on a pile of new-mown hay, soft yet buoyant. Wuntvor couldn't imagine a better seat.

The lad smiled. It was time to turn his attention to the food. There were three pieces of pie before him, the filling a tempting pinkish-purple. Cautiously, Wuntvor reached for the largest piece.

He pulled his hand back with a stifled cry, stuffing his fingers in his mouth. He had never in his life felt anything that hot! He examined his fingers. There didn't seem to be any permanent damage. And the juice that had clung to his skin had been quite tasty.

Even more cautiously, Wuntvor decided to touch another piece of the treacherous dessert. He pushed gently at the crust of the middle-sized piece. The crust didn't give at all. It was solid as a rock. And cold, too, as if someone had kept it stored in a mound of snow. Never in his life had he felt a dessert that cold.

The lad withdrew his hand. What was going on here? If he hadn't been so hungry, he would have left this strange place at that instant. But here he was, sitting on the smallest, most comfortable stool. As long as he was here, he might as well attempt to sample the smallest of the three wedges of pie.

He gently touched the crust. To the lad's surprise, it was pleasantly warm. He pulled the pie toward him. At last, he could satisfy his hunger. He took the wedge in both hands and brought it to his eager lips, tentatively sampling a bit of the filling with his tongue. It was delicious, just the right mixture of tart and sweet. There would be no more tricks this time.

Wuntvor took a big bite and screamed. He spit the contents of his mouth back onto the table. The pie was full of tiny sharp things, like nettles. A couple had gotten stuck to his tongue and gums, and the lad carefully pulled them out, whimpering softly with the pain. Who lived in this place anyway? Who would be crazy enough to bake a deadly pie?

That's when the lad heard the voices, and the heavy footsteps. Someone, more than one— two or three—they were coming into the cave!

Wuntvor jumped from the stool. Where could he go? Where could he hide? The voices were getting closer. They were just beyond the bend. The lad ran around the table and bolted through an open doorway that led into another room.

He looked quickly around this new space. Besides a small hole in the ceiling to let in light, there were no further openings. Wuntvor was trapped! But wait a moment. On the far side of the room were three pools. Perhaps one of them might lead to safety.

The voices were in the next room! Wuntvor ran to the wall by the door, praying whoever had arrived would not look in here until he had made his decision.

A deep, gravelly voice spoke first:

> "Guxx Unfufadoo, poppa demon,
> Sees that we've had an intruder!
> Sees that someone has been sitting
> In his stool—my rocks are messy!"

"Oh, dear—," another deep voice began, but stopped to cough. "Oh, dear," the same voice repeated, this time in a falsetto, "Someone's been sitting in my stool, too. Look, it's all saggy!"

"Someone's been sitting on my stool, too!" exclaimed a third voice, even more grating than the first two. "And the seat's still warm!"

Uh-oh, the lad thought. They suspected he was still here. If he was going to escape, it would have to be soon. But which of the three pools should he try? From what had already happened in this place, he knew he had to be careful. There could be all sorts of things lurking in those dark waters. As quietly as possible, the lad crept across the room, eager to examine his potential escape routes.

The deep voice spoke again in the other room:

> "Guxx Unfufadoo, poppa demon,
> Sees the stranger has not rested;
> Sees he's disturbed my Sweet Demon
> Pie—he's scuffed its molten surface!"

"Someone has touched my Sweet Demon Pie as well," the falsetto voice answered. "You can see the fingerprint etched in the frost. And I had put in extra brambles, just for you!"

"Someone's gone after my pie, too," said the most grating of the voices, "and— ptuui! —is he a messy eater!"

The voices in the other room were becoming more agitated by the minute. Wuntvor knew he would have to make a decision soon, or it would be too late. He knelt down by the largest of the three pools, trying to see whether it had a bottom.

The water appeared totally opaque. More than that, it looked like it was colored a dull gray. More even than that, Wuntvor doubted it was water at all, but rather some far heavier, more odiferous liquid. He wondered if he should disturb the surface with his hand, but was wary of the great quantities of steam the pool seemed to be producing. After all, he had already been burned once. No, this pool definitely would not do. Perhaps, he thought, he should try one of the others.

He duck-walked over to the next smaller of the three, but noticed that its surface was marred by something solid floating through the viscous liquid. It was only when the cold breeze rose to brush his face that he realized the solid particles were ice.

No, Wuntvor thought, that pool won't do either.

Still, there was the smallest of the three. So far in this household, he seemed to have the most luck with the most diminutive objects he had found. Perhaps his good fortune would hold here as well.

Cautiously, he placed his hand gently in the liquid. It slid down quickly, as if his flesh had somehow grown heavier under the surface. He imagined, if he had not braced himself, that not only his hand but the rest of him would have been drawn into the pool instantly. There was something strange about the feel of the liquid itself, too, somehow slippery and heavy at the same time, like oily oatmeal.

Wuntvor quickly pulled his fist from the pool. His hand was covered with slime.

"Uck!" the lad yelled, quite beside himself.

"Who's that?" three gruff voices called from the other room.

Wuntvor heard three sets of feet heading for the doorway. This, then, was his last chance to escape. He looked back at the mucous-filled pool. If he was going to jump, it was now or never.

Mucous-filled pool? The lad decided it would definitely be never.

He almost reconsidered when three heads appeared in the door.

"Guxx Unfufadoo, poppa demon,"

An incredibly large and ugly bluish-purple creature began,

Sees the stranger came in this way,
Sees she looked at all the slime pools,
Who's been mucking in our pool muck!"

The second demon nodded its somewhat shorter, somewhat grayer head, which caused its long hair to bob about like a gaggle of spastic snakes. That is, if you could call it hair. It looked to Wuntvor more like a mass of tangled seaweed.

"Someone dragged herself past my slime pit as well," the second creature added in its falsetto.

"Somebody's been inspecting my slime pit, too!" the third,

slightly smaller creature (who was wearing a lace bonnet) declared as it pointed at the cowering Wuntvor. "And there she is!"

She? the lad wondered for an instant, before he remembered his disguise.

"It's a human!" the lace bonneted demon continued. "And it might be female!"

The seaweed-haired creature waved pleasantly. "Welcome to our home, oh golden locks. As we are civilized creatures, I thought I might introduce the three of us before we eat you."

It pointed at the largest of the three. "This is the poppa demon. And over here is our little baby demon. And I, of course, am the momma demon." The seaweed-haired creature gave Wuntvor a conspiratorial glance. "Should you be interested, in this time of crisis, I also sell used weapons on the side."

With that, the poppa demon sauntered into the room.

> "Guxx Unfufadoo, poppa demon
> Sees our golden-haired intruder;
> Cooks her with a little butter;
> Eats her with a side of cole slaw!"

"Poppa's right," momma demon agreed pleasantly as it, too, entered the room. It was wearing a dress of orange and green plaid. "How fortunate that you have come. We really like to eat golden-haired girls."

"Even golden-haired girls that look like that?" baby demon sneered as it also hopped into the room. Wuntvor thought its diaper looked a little incongruous on one so green and scaly.

"Now, now, baby demon," momma reprimanded. "Diners can't be choosers." The creature smiled at Wuntvor. "Now, if you would just walk this way, I think I have a pot barely big enough!"

Wuntvor fought down the panic growing deep inside him. These were intelligent creatures, he told himself. Certainly they could be reasoned with.

"Indeed?" he asked. "And what if I was not exactly as I appeared? What if I were, say, an adventurer in disguise?"

"What if you were thrown into a pool of molten slime by an enraged demon?" the baby of the family replied. "It's not nice to fool poppa demon."

"Yes," the momma agreed, "Daddy does have a temper. But you won't have to worry about that, will you?" The creature frowned contemplatively at Wuntvor. "I'd say forty-five minutes at 375 degrees and all your worries will be over."

"Indeed," the lad replied, following the momma demon through the doorway into the other room. He reasoned that, though he would be much closer to the stove, he would also be that much closer to the cave mouth and escape.

"You can just sit anywhere." The momma demon motioned expansively at the glittering countertop before them. "Oh, and as long as you're sitting here, you wouldn't mind helping me peel carrots, would you? Believe me, it will help you pass the time." The creature opened a cupboard door and searched through a pile of large knives. It extracted the smallest of the lot and handed it apologetically to Wuntvor. "It's so hard to get good help down in these caves."

Wuntvor took the knife and began to peel. He wondered if he could use this little tool as a weapon. But what could he do with something this tiny—poke the demons to death?

It was then he recalled he still had a sword hiding under all his hair.

The momma demon chatted on as it minced onions. "I know that this may seem to be an imposition, in that we're going to eat you and all, but could you tell me who does your hair? I mean, look at mine! I can't do a thing with it. Lucky for my sideline. Amazing how a collection of used weapons cuts down on comments on your appearance."

"Uh—indeed," Wuntvor answered, keeping the conversation alive until he could think of a way to escape. "Mine just sort of—uh—comes naturally."

The momma demon sighed. "Well, I guess beautiful hair simply doesn't fall out of the sky. If you've got it, you've got it."

"We want to eat!" the baby demon exclaimed as it rushed into the room. The amazingly large and imposing poppa demon was right behind.

Well, the lad thought, it was now or never. He drew his sword with a scream.

"Oh, no you don't!" he shouted at the startled demons.

"That's right!" the sword added. "You don't. In fact, as of this moment, no one does!"

The lad stared at the sword. "I beg your pardon?"

"I've had enough of being whipped from my scabbard on a moment's notice!" the weapon sniffed haughtily. "From this minute on, I'm on strike! That's quite correct: As of now, I refuse to cut anything, anywhere, for any purpose. Sorry I have to be so blunt about this, but things have to change!"

"But I am about to be cooked and eaten!" the lad wailed.

"Sorry," the sword answered, "but your scare tactics won't work on me this time. You're always about to get killed one way or another. There comes a point when a weapon has to say 'no more'!"

Wuntvor looked up helplessly as the three demons approached.

"Do you have any last requests?" the momma demon asked as she raised her butcher knife.

The lad nodded. "Only one. I wish I could get out of this alive."

"Granted!" shouted a tiny voice from nowhere.

TEN

The practicing wizard will often find himself in stressful situations. Two different clients may expect completely opposite results from some magical situation. The practicing mage must therefore weight each client's case carefully, thinking of the long-term results of his magicks, what part of his spells will best satisfy each client, and how best to leave if one of the parties in question becomes angered by the results. But no matter what the outcome, the practicing wizard must never neglect the first rule of professional wizardry: Always make sure you are paid by both clients well in advance.

— *The Teachings of Ebenezum*, VOLUME XXI

Wuntvor found himself back in the forest. The Brownie stood beside him.

"See?" the sword in his hands reproached him. "There are always alternatives to violence."

The lad slid his weapon back into its scabbard. He would have to deal with it later.

"So where have you been?" the lad demanded of the little fellow.

"Oh, here and there," the Brownie replied nonchalantly. "I've always been there when you needed me, haven't I? We wee folk have ways of making ourselves scarce. I decided that my presence was getting in the way of your story. It's an area of concern for us magic-producers: You were becoming too wish-conscious."

"My story?" Somehow, the lad had never thought of his adventures in quite that way. Still, why else would he keep saying "Once upon a time"?

"But now it's time for me to come back," the Brownie explained. "It's the Grande Finale. You've only got one wish left. You'd better make this one a doozy."

For a minute, Wuntvor considered wishing for a pudding and getting it over with once and for all. But no, with the way his luck had been running lately, he would probably need the last wish for something serious. He told the Brownie to stick around.

"As you wish," the little fellow replied, adding quickly: "Sorry, just a manner of speaking."

The lad turned from the Brownie to examine his surroundings. He was once again near the huge beanstalk, although now the giant seemed to be nowhere about. In fact, nothing much had changed, save for a sizable depression in the forest floor that Wuntvor had not noticed before.

"Indeed," the lad remarked after a moment's thought. "I think it is time for me to resume my escape."

But he had not gone a dozen steps before a chorus of voices assailed him from the surrounding shrubbery.

"Your mother wears army boots!" the first voice yelled.

"That's exactly like a human," a second voice added. "We come to visit, and you don't even say hello!"

"Oh, wow!" a third voice commented.

Eight very short men stepped from the forest and formed a semi-circle around them.

"Indeed?" Wuntvor asked. "Pardon me, but have we met?"

One of the eight stepped forward, and spoke as he wrung his hands. "Oh dear, oh my. Excuse us, please. We didn't realize you were still under one of Mother Duck's spells. We are, of course, the Seven Other Dwarves." He waved to his fellows. "Snooty, Nasty, Touchy, Dumpy, Noisy, Sickly and

Spacey. And I am their humble and only barely competent leader, Smarmy."

"You can say that again!" one of the other dwarves shouted. Wuntvor assumed that must be Nasty. Unless he was Snooty?

"And who elected you?" another asked with a tone of moral outrage. Okay, then this one must be Snooty. Unless he was Touchy?

One of the others groaned. Did that mean he was Noisy? Or could he be Dumpy or Sickly? Wuntvor decided that this speculation was getting him nowhere.

"Indeed," he began. "It's been awfully nice chatting with you, but unfortunately, I was in the midst of escaping."

"But that is the very reason we are here!" Smarmy exclaimed, redoubling his hand wringing. "How serendipitous for all of us!"

"Pardon," said the lad, quite surprised. "Are you escaping as well?"

"What a stupid idea!" one of the others, who had to be Nasty, replied.

"If you will excuse the forwardness of my fellow dwarf," Smarmy interjected, "no, escape is the farthest thing from our minds. As magical creatures, we belong in the Eastern Kingdoms. Rather, we have been sent by Norei, to help guide you in your own escape."

Norei? His beloved! The beautiful witch's face came back to Wuntvor in a rush. It was hazy still, he realized with a shiver. What else had he forgotten?

"That is correct," Smarmy continued after Wuntvor had regained his equilibrium. "Now please listen carefully, and may I say that I am honored that one as unworthy as myself was chosen to pass on this information—"

Smarmy paused for a second as catcalls like "You can say that again *twice!*" and "Yeah, who *did* pick you to be leader?" emanated from his fellows before he continued:

"You are to go to a hill in the west, and wait there for His Brownieship."

"His Brownieship?" Tap, the Brownie wish-giver, suddenly paled.

"But Norei—," Wuntvor began, desiring to see the young witch as soon as possible.

"I must beg your forgiveness," Smarmy interrupted, "but

that is all I know. You must travel to the Western hill."

"His Brownieship?" the little fellow fretted. "Why would he be coming here, when I'm already in charge? I mean, I've been doing my job, haven't I?" The Brownie frowned up at Wuntvor. "Oh, dear. Maybe I haven't. What is this seven wishes thing, anyway?" He hit his tiny cheek with his tiny hand. "Mother Duck! I've fallen under her spells!" He appeared to be sweating. He tugged earnestly at Wuntvor's sackcloth skirt.

"Listen," he said to the lad, "I'd appreciate it if you didn't mention anything that's happened lately when His Brownieship shows up. I mean—buckles and laces!—I'll be demoted to heel sorting!"

"Indeed?" the lad agreed, not absolutely clear himself on all the fine points of what had happened. "What say we resume our escape?" If there was one thing he was sure of, it was that, if Norei had asked him to do so, he wanted to get to that western hill as soon as possible!

"Farewell, then!" Smarmy called as Wuntvor and Tap marched to the west. "And believe me, I can't wait for this to be over so that I can resume my Brownie lessons."

"Oh, that." The Brownie grinned sheepishly. "Perhaps, if it's all right with you, we won't mention that to His Brownieship either." The little fellow groaned softly, shaking his head. "I'll be demoted to bent buckle straightening!"

The Brownie had to hurry to catch up with the marching Wuntvor, who was rushing so fast that he almost tripped over his skirt at least three times. The small steps, indeed, the whole charade was forgotten in the lad's hurry to see Norei again. He had to reach that hill before Mother Duck's spell could reassert itself. He had to! Nothing would get in his way this time!

The day was growing late, the forest around them filled with long shadows. Wuntvor picked the Brownie up so that he might move even faster, heedless of the bushes and shrubs that stood in his way. They came at last to a clearing, but they both had to squint to make out a large shape etched against the glare of the late afternoon sun.

"Is that the hill we seek?" he asked the Brownie.

Tap still squinted into the brightness. At last he spoke, his voice hushed: "Alas, no. It is something even more awe-inspiring."

The Brownie climbed to Wuntvor's shoulder and whispered in his ear. "It is a shoe."

The lad stared at the shape. A shoe that big could mean only one thing—

"Oops!" came from far overhead.

A copse was smashed to splinters directly behind them.

"Now just stand still!" Richard the giant called down to them. "It's not going to do you any good to run. I'm too big to get away from!"

Wuntvor resisted the urge to flee screaming into the forest. He knew the giant was right, and furthermore, he suspected that, the more he might try to escape Richard, the larger the risk would become of falling victim to one of the huge fellow's frequent accidents.

The giant scooped the lad up in one very large hand.

"Ah," his very large voice boomed with satisfaction. "I knew I'd get you sooner or later!" He brought his hand up to eye level, peering intently at the lad. "Not that it's any of my business, but why are you wearing that silly costume?"

Wuntvor couldn't take it. It was the final straw. He would go down fighting! He pulled his sword.

"All right!" Cuthbert demanded hysterically. "What's going on this time?"

"We have to take on a giant," the lad replied.

"A giant?" the sword asked a bit too brightly. "Oh, is that all? Why don't we take on the entire amassed might of the Netherhells, instead? Oh, I forgot. We've already done that! And, speaking of forgetting, I suppose you don't remember our conversation from the last time I was out of the scabbard?"

The lad's brow crinkled with thought. "That was when we were with the demons?"

"Bravo," the sword replied sarcastically. "There's something about constantly being trapped in these fairy tales. It sure wreaks havoc with the continuity!"

"Indeed," Wuntvor responded. "I fear we have no time for continuity, or naught else but battle!"

"See?" the sword cried with a note of triumph. "You don't

remember! Well, I guess I'll have to fill you in again. I'm on strike!"

"Pardon?" the lad inquired.

"I quit," Cuthbert affirmed. "My life should be more than hacking and slashing. I must have complained to you about this a hundred times, and still you wouldn't listen. Well, there comes a point when a magic sword must take a stand. As of this moment, my fighting days are through. Not another cut! Not another parry! And riposting is completely out of the question."

The lad stared at the sword. "Indeed? Well, if that is the way you feel."

"Who are you talking to?" the giant rumbled, peering at the tiny man in his hand.

"Oh, nothing. Something completely beneath your notice."

"What?" Cuthbert demanded. "I expected you to negotiate. Instead I become nothing?"

The lad shrugged. "How do I explain a sword that won't cut or parry? It seems to me that the object in question ceases to be a sword."

"You are too talking to something," the giant rumbled.

"Well," Cuthbert said, considering the lad's words, "perhaps my reaction has been a little extreme. I suppose I could agree to a concession or two. I mean, I'm a reasonable sword. Say, I might consent to a little dueling here and there—you know, in demonstrations and charity jousts—things like that."

"No, no, I assure you," Wuntvor insisted to the giant. "This whole thing is beneath your notice."

"Beneath his notice!" the sword wailed. "Oh, you're a tough negotiator. All right, because we've been together so long, I'll even do a *real* swordfight once in a while, one-on-one, duels of honor between gentlemen, as long as there's no bloodshed."

Richard frowned. "Won't you tell me, please? I'm tired of missing things beneath my notice. Being a giant, you miss a lot of the nitty gritty."

"All right! All right!" the sword blurted. "All right, perhaps even a little blood now and then, as long as you clean me quickly. Only, no ichor! I refuse to do ichor!"

"This is my magic sword," Wuntvor told the giant.

"Thank you," Cuthbert commented.

Richard flinched. "That isn't anything like a magic toothpick, is it?"

"Well, a bit. Except a sword is, of course, much more powerful." He had disabled the giant with a magic toothpick once before, he remembered. But he neglected to mention that, unlike the toothpick, the sword lacked the ability to grow to a size large enough to bother the giant.

"I don't know if this is fair," the big fellow complained. "You have to promise not to use that thing."

Wuntvor shook his head. "I don't promise anything, unless you put us back down."

The giant's frown deepened even further. "Put you down? I don't think Mother Duck would like that."

"Indeed?" Wuntvor replied regretfully. "I may have to use the sword. . . ."

"Now wait a minute—," Cuthbert began.

"That is," Wuntvor whispered, "if I had a sword."

"Use the sword! Use the sword!" the weapon insisted.

"Hey!" Tap called, still perched on Wuntvor's shoulder. "Don't forget you have another weapon."

"More voices," Richard grumbled. "Why do all you people have to be so small?"

Wuntvor glanced over at the little fellow. "Tap," he whispered, "do you really think you could work some magic on this giant's shoes?"

"You mean those?" Tap pointed at the footwear far below. He looked back at Wuntvor, wonder in his eyes. "If I do this right, it could be my masterpiece!"

"You're not answering my questions!" Richard rumbled. "Giants are not used to being ignored. Not that I want to provoke you into using your sword—anything but that. It's just that someone as large as I am expects civil conversation from my victims."

Tap concentrated, a terrible frown on his tiny face.

"What?" the giant demanded. "What's happening to my shoes?"

The Brownie began a slow dance from Wuntvor's collarbone to his shoulder socket.

"Hey!" the giant cried. His tone had become threatening. "You remember Mother Duck's ovens, don't you? What's happening to my laces?"

Tap's dance became more sprightly. Wuntvor winced at the pounding of tiny feet, but did his best not to move. Brownie Power was their only hope.

"My shoes! My shoes are moving!" The giant swallowed, a distant booming sound, as he tried to regain his composure. "Yes, the ovens! The ones where she bakes heroes into bread?"

Tap redoubled his jumping about, adding rhythmic hand gestures.

"Well—," the giant gasped, rivers of sweat now exploding from his enormous brow. "Well, you're about to become a hero sandwi—" The huge fellow breathed in sharply. "I can't stand it anymore! I've gotta dance!"

And with that, Richard began leaping about, clumsily mimicking the Brownie's movements. Wuntvor fell into the giant's palm, clinging for dear life.

"Oops," Tap gasped, clinging in turn to Wuntvor's wig. "Perhaps I overdid it."

"Indeed," Wuntvor agreed, watching the scenery move wildly as the giant swung his hand from shoulder level up above his head. "I suppose you can't undo this?"

The Brownie shook his head, miserable. "I'm afraid not. I mean, how can you undance?"

The lad looked below them, his expression grim. "Then we're going to have to jump."

"Jump?" the Brownie wailed.

Wuntvor pointed at the huge head below. "Into his hair! Now!"

Both lad and Brownie leapt. The hair bounced beneath them, breaking their fall. Wuntvor slid down a thick strand, waving for Tap to follow.

A moment later, they had both planted their feet firmly on the giant's skull. Wuntvor looked about him. From here, Richard's hair looked like a dense, dark forest, save that the hair had a much rougher exterior than any tree bark, and was covered with a thick, moist substance.

Tap inspected the moisture more closely, wrinkling his nose. "Hair oil."

"Indeed," the lad replied as he caught his breath. The giant continued to jump around beneath them. "Pray tell me, Tap, what will happen when the dance is over?"

"Why," Tap replied proudly, "the dance is never over. The recipient of the dancing spell dances on and on, until—"

The Brownie paused, a look of horror on his tiny countenance.

"Until?" the lad prompted.

"Exhaustion!" the Brownie whispered.

The skull lurched wildly beneath them.

"Quickly!" Wuntvor cried. "Into my pocket, Tap! We must anchor ourselves." He pulled forth his sword.

"What is it *this* time?" Cuthbert screamed.

"No blood!" the lad called back. "We just need to stick you in this giant hair follicle."

"That oily thing? Yu—" The weapon's voice died as its point gushed into the spongy strand. The Brownie leapt for the protection of the lad's vest.

Richard swayed a final time, then stumbled to his knees. Wuntvor swung wildly about, but the sword held.

"Gotta—," the giant managed, his labored breath as loud as the wind between two mountaintops,"—dance." And with that, the giant collapsed, falling face first to the earth far below.

"Oops," Richard mumbled, his nose and brow pressed against the shattered pine trees. Then he began to snore.

Wuntvor stood, shaken but still more or less in one piece. He pulled Cuthbert free from the oily stalk.

"—uck!" the sword concluded. "I had thought there was nothing worse than ichor. Apparently I was wrong."

Wuntvor sheathed the weapon before it could complain further. He climbed carefully down from strand to strand, careful not to slip on the moist hair. He breathed a sigh of relief as his feet finally touched the ground.

Tap peered out of the lad's pocket.

"Are we down yet?"

Wuntvor nodded, still catching his breath.

"Totally off the giant?" Tap asked. "Completely on the ground?"

"Indeed," the lad answered.

Tap leapt from Wuntvor's pocket with a flourish. He did a

little dance as his tiny feet hit the earth, waving at the fallen giant. "I tell you, was that Brownie Power or what?"

"Indeed," Wuntvor said again, rather than what he was really thinking. "I wonder if we have gotten any closer to the western hill?" In fact, Richard's head seemed to have crashed into a rise of some sort. It was so hard to tell. The giant's head was so big, it made everything else seem disproportionately small.

There was a small explosion directly in front of them.

"His Brownieship!" Tap exclaimed.

"I'll deal with you later," the newcomer replied. For it was, indeed, the King of the Brownies, complete with his leather crown. Tap moaned softly, fearing the worst.

"But first," His Brownieship announced regally, "I have a message. And I am better at delivering messages than some Brownies I know." Tap moaned again, covering his tiny head with his tiny hands.

His Brownieship looked up at Wuntvor. "There are shoes in your future."

"Indeed?" the lad queried.

The King of the Brownies nodded nobly. "Very big shoes."

"You might be a little late." Wuntvor pointed down at the other end of the giant. "Would those be the shoes you mean?"

His Brownieship frowned, then leapt up to Wuntvor's shoulder to get a better view. He stared for a long moment, speechless.

The Brownie king tore his gaze away at last. "No, those are not the shoes." His head turned once again toward the giant. "Still, they may require further study—" His Brownieship shook himself. "But this is not the time. I have told you what I dare. In the Eastern Kingdoms, Mother Duck is everywhere. You will know the shoe when you see it. Norei and I will attempt to distract—but I have already said too much. Just remember— Happily ever after!"

Happily ever after? The unicorn had told him about that, too, but what with all the excitement in dealing with Richard, the phrase had slipped the young lad's mind.

"Indeed," Wuntvor agreed.

"And now," His Brownieship continued, turning his attention to Tap, "as to what we will do to certain Brownies who apparently find it impossible to follow orders . . ."

"Buckles and laces!" Tap pleaded. "But, Your Smallness, there were extenuating circumstances!"

"Circumstances that led you to completely forget you were supposed to wait for me in Vushta?" His Brownieship demanded.

"Well—uh—yes," Tap replied somewhat unevenly. "You see, there was this quest, and this demon, Snarks, whom I was supposed to teach the wisdom of the Brownie Way, and then these Seven Other Dwarves—"

A horrible, deep rumbling noise drowned out the Brownie's excuses. It took Wuntvor a moment to realize what the noise was: Richard had groaned.

"And I suppose," His Brownieship spoke to Tap as if the giant wasn't even there, "you also completely forgot the Brownie Code when you got wrapped up in this silly seven wishes thing?"

"Well, you see, then we ended up in the Eastern Kingdoms," Tap continued hurriedly. The little fellow seemed to be perspiring even more heavily than he had during his giant-controlling dance. "You can't imagine how powerful Mother Duck is. And then there was this giant, see—"

The earth moved as the giant sat up.

"Oops," Richard intoned. "I didn't mean to fall down like that. But at least you weren't so foolish as to run away. Nobody can run away from a giant."

Wuntvor drew his sword.

"Don't I get any rest at all?" Cuthbert wailed. "It's bad enough that I'm still all slimy from hair oil!"

"I'm still waiting for an answer," His Brownieship said to his subordinate.

"All right now," Richard remarked as he shifted his weight. "I want you all down there to stay calm. Let's make this capture as painless as possible."

"Indeed," Wuntvor remarked. "Tap, perhaps your best answer would be to repeat the Brownie Power dance that defeated the giant before."

"Buckles and laces!" Tap exclaimed, looking anxiously at His Brownieship. "Would that be all right?"

"Of course," Richard continued, "I can't guarantee you a painless future. Who knows what Mother Duck has in store? After all, bread may be your destiny."

"That would be better than being stuck in a scabbard when you're covered with slime!" Cuthbert commented. "And after all the service I've given you. Don't you ever think of cleaning your weapon?"

Richard frowned. "That's that magic sword again, isn't it? I warned you about that magic sword!"

"Yes," Wuntvor hissed to Tap. "I think it is once again time for Brownie Power!"

"Is it?" Tap whimpered to His Brownieship.

"Perhaps," the Brownie king replied coolly. "After you have given me an account of all your actions."

"Is there anything in Brownie Power that can clean off hair oil?" Cuthbert asked hopefully.

"You've heard my warning," Richard rumbled. "Here I come."

Tap stared at the descending hand, then turned wildly to the others.

"Do something!" Wuntvor pleaded.

"Explain!" His Brownieship demanded.

"Do nothing!" the giant warned.

"Clean me off!" the sword moaned.

"That's it!" Tap the Brownie shrieked. "I can't take it anymore! Once upon a time. Once upon a time!"

A glazed look came over the Brownie's countenance. The worried, perspiring Tap was gone. Wuntvor realized that in his place was a calm, collected little person, totally under the control of Mother Duck.

"What's happening here?" His Brownieship demanded. Tap didn't respond. The Brownie king turned angrily to Wuntvor.

"If I don't get this oil cleaned off me, I'm going back on strike," Cuthbert complained. "I demand decent working conditions!"

"Now I want you to stay perfectly still," Richard said quietly. "We don't want any accidents. You know how easy it would be for me to squeeze just a little too hard." The giant made a *tsk*ing sound that resembled distant thunder. "You'd be turned into pumpernickel in no time."

"I'm warning you!" The Brownie king shook his tiny fist at Wuntvor. "I need to know what happened to Tap. His Brownieship does not like to be fooled! I demand an answer!"

"So do I!" echoed the sword.

Wuntvor was beginning to realize the feelings that had driven Tap to his present state.

The giant's hand was almost on top of him.

"Very good," Richard the giant rumbled. "No resistance at all. That's a good victim."

Wuntvor was almost beyond his wit's end. He had to say something.

"Enough!" he screamed. "I wish I didn't have to deal with any of you people!"

"Granted!" Tap the Brownie shouted with finality.

Wuntvor knew immediately that he had made a mistake.

ELEVEN

S *is for the sole that goes on forward,*
H *is for the heel that rearwards be,*
O *is for the oxen-leather stitching,*
E *is for the eyelets, don't you see?*
Put them all together, they spell SHOE-oo,
And that means an awful lot to me!

—*The Brownie Creed,* Stanza 603

I knew I was in trouble the moment I opened my eyes. Without thinking, I had wished myself away from all the others, and apparently, completely out of Mother Duck's control. But where had I wished myself to?

I still was in a forest, perhaps in another part of the Eastern Woods. But it was different here, far darker than the clearing where we had met the giant. The trees were much taller and broader, towering far overhead, their great shadows keeping the sunlight from the forest floor. Their bark was dark gray as well, almost the gray of the shadows, and for a moment I imagined I had wished myself to a place that held no color, but only shades of shadow.

I tilted my head back as far as I could, trying to see the tops of those monstrous trees. There, high overhead, I could see some small patches of blue. But the color gave me no comfort because of what else I saw above me.

Here it was, the end of summer, and none of the trees had leaves. Their branches were barren, shaking in the wind high overhead, rattling against one another like skeleton bones. All the trees were dead.

That same breeze whipped against me with an unexpected suddenness, blowing Alea's borrowed blond hair from my head. I let it go. The giant had seen through my disguise in an instant. I pulled the sackcloth skirt up about my shoulders, hoping the extra fabric would provide me with some protection against the sudden chill.

I did not like this; it was all too familiar. I had been in a forest like this before.

I thought I heard a dry chuckle carried by the wind.

I turned and saw a robed figure regarding me from between the trees. Even before I could see his face through the shadows, I knew what to expect; the darkened sockets, the skull-like grin, the hands that looked like whitened bones.

"Greetings," the sepulchral voice of Death announced as the spectre approached. "It has been quite some time, Eternal Apprentice, since we have had a chance to speak alone."

I stood my ground as Death drew nearer, floating toward me as if he was carried forward by the howling wind rather than anything as simply mortal as legs and feet. Death seemed to think there was something special about me. That was why he called me the "Eternal Apprentice," a soul that managed to elude Death's grasp by constantly being reborn in new forms, a soul destined to always aid, however clumsily, true heroes, with the assistance of multiple companions.

I had no idea if there was any truth in Death's claim. But it didn't seem to matter what I thought about it. Death had decided that I had somehow escaped his kingdom many times in past lives, and because of that he was willing to bend the rules of life and death, and steal me away as soon as I was alone.

As I was now. All alone with Death, without even my cowardly sword to protect me.

Death grinned at me, and held out his hand. "You cannot imagine how I have longed for this moment. To at last possess the one who has forever been beyond my grasp!"

He threw his head back and laughed, a high-pitched, frightening sound, like nightbirds falling from the sky with broken wings.

"Indeed," I responded, concentrating mightily to keep my voice from cracking in terror. Death would take me now; he had made his desire for my Eternal Apprentice soul abundantly clear in my last two narrow escapes. But I could not succumb to the emotions that raged inside me, threatening to block my windpipe, to stop my heart. Perhaps, I reasoned instead, if I could get Death to talk, he might betray some weakness and inadvertently show me a way to save myself.

"Indeed?" Death replied, a bit surprised.

"Indeed," I said again. "I think not."

Death chuckled, the sound of black beetles being ground underfoot.

"Pitiful human," the spectre whispered. "Resistance is useless against a force such as Death. Still, you know my fondness for games. Come! Try your best to keep me from taking you to my kingdom of darkness, and I will thank you for giving me my sport."

I took a step away. Somehow, though I did not see him move, Death seemed no farther away than before. If anything, he was closer; his outstretched hand now almost touched my shoulder.

"You will not escape that way," the spectre said. "Death is everywhere." He flexed his bone-white fingers. "Come now. Take my hand. It will be so simple."

Was this, then, the end? I could feel panic shooting up my spine. Before, my companions had always rushed to my aid, presenting Death with far too many souls to dispose of, thus defeating his deadly plans. Now, though, I was completely alone, far from everyone I knew. I had even lost my trusty ferret, in an earlier altercation with the giant. The silence of the dead forest seemed to close in around me. Oh, if I could only hear that reassuring "Eep-eep-eep" which had saved me from Death before.

Death's bony fingers brushed the cloth at my shoulder.

"No!" I cried. "I am not ready!"

Death guffawed, the sound vultures make as they circle their prey. "Ready? You don't have to be ready for Death. It simply happens. Come now. I have plagues to spread, disasters to provoke. Death can never rest."

His hand reached for me again. "Come! No one can resist me!"

I am not precisely sure what happened next. The soft, barren earth beneath my feet seemed to give way as I kicked back from the reach of Death. The ground appeared to slip one way, my boots another. Whatever the cause, I lost my footing. I looked up to see Death grasp the empty air where once my head had been.

"I have never seen anyone so clumsy!" the spectre raged. "And you would dare to deny you are the Eternal Apprentice!"

I rolled away, scrambling to my feet.

"Indeed," I remarked, searching for some words that might further distract the angry spectre.

"What is that?" Death whispered in a voice as cold as Midwinter Night.

I stopped, and in the stillness I, too, heard something cry, an animal of some sort, coming toward us!

"Eep!" the animal sounded. "Eep! Eep!"

I knew what it was even before I saw its gray form streaking between the trees.

It was my ferret.

"Eep!" the ferret cried, overjoyed to see me. "Eep! Eep!"

Death stared at the ferret in disbelief. "That is impossible. We are in the most destitute part of the Eastern Woods, miles from life of any kind. And yet, you are sought out by this animal companion. And still you doubt that you are the Eternal Apprentice?"

The ferret leapt up into my arms. I, too, believed it was a great coincidence that my pet could find me, out in the midst of these barren woods. But then again, this was one of my magic ferrets, produced from an equally magic hat I had taken with me to the Netherhells. Perhaps, because I had conjured them, the ferrets were somehow connected to me. Could it be, then, that all I had to do was think of them, and they would come?

Death glowered at the ferret, spreading his arms wide as if he would encircle me in a skeletal hug.

"Before, I would have contented myself to merely touch you," the spectre leered. "But no, you choose to elude my deadly grasp.. Now, I will be forced to wrestle you to the ground. I will take your soul, and the life of that ferret, too! Submit, mortal! No one can survive the grip of Death!"

I am also not entirely clear on the exact sequence of subsequent events, but I do remember Death lunging for me again and the ferret streaking between us, and my arms flailing to get out of the way, but despite my best efforts somehow getting caught up in Death's robes, and the spectre flying over my head, falling to the ground with a rattle of bones. I tried to scramble away, only to have my feet get caught by the robes' coarse material.

Death managed to roll away at last, freeing his ripped robes from my heavy boots.

"This cannot be happening!" the spectre screamed. "I can see it all now: You will stumble around, barely eluding capture, until the entire world happens to wander into this corner of the forest!" Death laughed ruefully, the sound of forest bears being slowly strangled.

There was another noise behind us.

"What was that?" Death shrieked as he whirled about. For some reason, he seemed to be losing his composure. "It can't be!"

I turned to look as well. It was a shoe that had made the noise. A very large shoe. For a moment, my heart stopped. Then I saw that it was perhaps not as large a shoe as it would take to fit a giant, but a shoe big enough to hide a mortal man.

"Indeed," the shoe stated.

"A shoe?" Death whispered. "More than that, a talking shoe? It cannot be, and yet it is." The spectre turned back to me, its voice gaining power with every word. "But, no matter what its true nature, I will not be foiled. I have come to take you this time, Eternal Apprentice, even though I may be tempting the forces of chaos to do so. It will be simple enough to take the ferret, too. And even though I am not quite sure what it is, the talking shoe is mine as well!"

"I think not," the shoe replied, as two hands emerged from the very large footwear's very large eyelets. The hands set themselves into prime conjuring position.

"A talking wizard shoe!" Death stared, and his voice was tinged with wonder. "Every once in a while, there is something that can surprise even me. But I will have all the time I desire to examine it, once it is mine. And I take the Eternal Apprentice, too!" The spectre chuckled once again. "What a day this will be for Death."

But the hands in the shoe had already begun to conjure, and, as they moved, a small, intensely dark cloud appeared over the spectre.

"How can you stop me?" Death asked in amusement. "Magic holds no power over me."

The hands waved again, and a great, jagged bolt of lightning streaked down upon the robed spectre, followed by a crash of thunder that almost shattered my ears.

I blinked, trying to regain the totality of my sight after the brightness of the lightning. A great cloud of dust had risen about where the spectre had once stood.

Then the chill winter wind howled all about us, blowing the dust away. Death stood there still. And his grin was, if anything, broader than ever.

"Is that all your pitiful magic can do?" The spectre waved at the dissipating cloud overhead. "You try to turn my own tools against me. I use the lightning for my sword, and the thunder heralds my approach. Foolish mortals, you will never defeat me that way!"

"Indeed?" the shoe remarked, obviously not impressed.

Death screamed at the impertinence.

"Wuntvor!" the shoe called. "Run to my side!"

I did as the shoe asked, for I knew that powerful voice. My master, the wizard Ebenezum, greatest mage in the Western Kingdoms, was inside. I turned around to look at Death, my back pressed reassuringly against the dark brown leather. The ferret, with a glad "eep," climbed to my shoulders.

The spectre approached, arms opened wide, as if he would

lift us all to his dark kingdom.

"Why do you bother to run? Why do you bother to conjure? All your plans, all your spells are as nothing to the Power of Death."

Death was coming fast. Surely my master could do something. I wondered if it would be better if I moved to the other side of the shoe, away from the ensuing battle. But when I stepped toward the heel, I saw a bone white hand before me. Death blocked my way. I was trapped against the shoe!

"At last," Death snickered, the sound of butterfly wings being torn apart by knives. "I have been waiting for this moment for ever so long."

"Oops!"

A large portion of the dead forest came crashing down nearby. Richard the giant had arrived.

"So here you are," Richard rumbled. "I wondered what all that noise was about."

"No!" Death screamed, the sound of a million souls in agony. "I will not be thwarted again. Though it will task my powers of attrition and decay, I will take all of you, shoe and giant, apprentice and ferret!" He smiled fiercely as he looked at all the living. "Prepare to die!"

"See?" a voice called overhead, accompanied by the heavy flapping of dragon's wings. "I knew with all that noise, there had to be something interesting happening."

"Yeah!" a woman's voice answered. "And Wuntie's here, too!"

There was a small popping sound close to my foot. "Hey!" a tiny voice said. "That explosion was almost louder than Brownie Power!"

"Nooooooo!" Death wailed, the sound of a hurricane laying waste to everything in its path. And then the spectre was gone as well.

"No, no, no, no, no!" Mother Duck rushed into our midst, followed closely by Jeffrey the Wolf. "This has gotten totally out of hand!"

"Well," Jeffrey added, "if you just would have taken my simple suggestions about the use of wolves . . ."

"I don't want to hear any more from you, either," she

snapped. "I had no idea, in dealing with the Eternal Apprentice, how complicated things could become!" She paused to smile. "Now, though, that I see the scope of the situation, I can *really* put you in a fairy tale!"

"Indeed," I said, stepping forward. "I think not." I found I had a new confidence, now that my master was here. "We have ways of dealing with you."

"Oh, really?" Mother Duck replied, already humbled by these new circumstances. "And what might they be?"

I waved behind me. "Well, for example, take a look at this shoe."

Mother Duck frowned. "What shoe? Are you standing on it or something? Shoes aren't all that big, you know."

What did she mean, "What shoe"? Was this one of Mother Duck's tricks? I spun around.

There was no longer a shoe behind me. In fact, the enormous footwear was nowhere to be seen.

My master was gone.

TWELVE

When you wish upon a star,
Wish for song and dance, and you'll go far.

> —*The Damsel and Dragon Songbook*
> (still seeking publication)

"There, there, now," Mother Duck spoke soothingly to my confusion. "I'm not surprised that you are a little addled, not after all that has happened. Don't worry, Mother Duck will not be cross with you. Especially since you have to work again so soon."

"Doom!" a deep voice echoed through the trees. "What have I missed?"

Mother Duck sighed as Hendrek bounded into our midst. "Apparently, everybody in the immediate vicinity will be arriving here shortly. I am quite in awe of the drawing power of the Eternal Apprentice." She patted me graciously on top of the head. "I've never gotten to use the spectre of Death in one of my fairy stories before. It's very impressive, the supporting cast that comes with you. And how you get out of these things!

Someday, you'll have to explain to me exactly how you made that sound.''

It occurred to me then that Mother Duck did not know about my master's arrival. Perhaps it was best kept secret, at least for now.

"Indeed," I said at last, for I felt the old woman expected an answer. "Perhaps I shall, when I am given more control over my own destiny."

"Oh, but I have been giving you more control." Mother Duck grinned congenially at me. "You and your companions had been fighting against me for so long, I decided to loosen the reins a wee bit. And when I did, I was rewarded by the occurrence of even wilder events. Of course, those events were almost completely out of hand, but we can fix that when we fine-tune the fairy tale later."

"Fine tune?" I asked, being unfamiliar with the term.

Mother Duck nodded enthusiastically. "It's a phrase we use in the fairy tale business. Fine-tune—fine-tuning—" She looked heavenward, as if searching for the precise words. "Yes, you know, improvements we add to the fairy tale as we continue to rehearse it, over and over, until we get it just right. It's going to take a bit longer than usual with all the variables. Still, I think thirty or forty run throughs should start us in the right direction."

"Thirty or forty?" I asked, afraid to further inquire just what constituted a "run through."

"Doom," Hendrek added.

''See how much easier it all becomes when you cooperate?'' Mother Duck enthused. ''With my fairy tale experience, and the incredible number of things that happen to you, I think we can make storytelling history here. That is why I gave you your own way a little more as we went along, while of course still supervising the action in case I might again need to take control.''

My own way? Taking control? Now that she mentioned it, I remembered how odd I had felt trying to escape the giant, as if I was somehow reading or hearing a story, rather than participating in it. It was only when I once again confronted Death that I truly felt my destiny once more under my own power.

Now, I realized that my taking charge of my own life was but a happy accident, and one that Mother Duck would soon rectify so that I might repeat the events of the past few hours another three dozen times. I also realized, with a new clarity, how important it was for Norei and Ebenezum to rescue me. If something didn't happen soon, I feared that I would spend the rest of my existence doomed to constantly relive a fairy tale full of seven Brownie wishes.

"It's about time we found you guys!" an incredibly grating voice called out as the three demons, who had apparently left their fairy tale bonnets and seaweed wigs behind, emerged from the trees.

"Might I make a suggestion?" Snarks called out as the three approached. "If you're going to blow up something to get our attention, next time why don't you do it a little closer to civilization?"

Get their attention? It was only there, in the midst of the crowd, that I realized my master's true intention in conjuring up the thunderstorm. Not to defeat Death with the lightning, but rather to overwhelm him with the crowd that would be attracted by the sound. I marveled at my master's foresight. He truly was the greatest wizard in the Western Kingdoms! I wondered in what clever way he would strike next.

Snarks looked around at the dead and broken trees. "Boy, you sure can pick some scenic spots to hold a meeting. Reminds me of some of the prime areas of the Netherhells; you know, urban renewal zones, sites of major industrial accidents."

"Begin!" Guxx Unfufadoo intoned. Brax hastily retrieved his drum from his ever-present sack.

> "Guxx Unfufadoo, angered demon,
>   Wants no more of fairy stories,
>   Warns the Mother if she uses
>   Demons more it will get gor—"

The large demon fell to the ground, overwhelmed by a sneezing fit.

"Such a shame," Brax murmured as he watched his indisposed leader roll about in the dust. "Such a natural rhyming talent, gone to waste."

"What?" Mother Duck stared at the thrashing demon. "What is going on here?"

"Indeed," I replied, trying to concoct a reasonable, but false, explanation. For it had occurred to me that not only did Mother Duck not know that my master, the great wizard Ebenezum, had magically traveled to her kingdom, she also did not know of my master's malady, similar in nature to that of the sneezing demon now rolling about before us. "Indeed," I therefore repeated, stalling for time. "Alas—uh—the poor demon tends to sneeze—uh—when he is—uh—overwrought."

"Really?" Mother Duck marveled. "From what I have seen, I thought he spent his entire life being overwrought. Still, that is useful information. I may be able to use it in one of my fairy tales."

"Indeed," I added for a final time. I looked about at my companions, urging them to complicity in my deceit. While the situation seemed to make the truth-telling Snarks uncomfortable, both Brax and Hubert nodded knowingly.

"What the demon needs to do is relax!" the dragon announced. "And what better way to relax than appreciating song and dance! Hit it, damsel! Number 703!"

"Always a winner!" Alea agreed. She made gentle shooing motions with her hands. "If all you folks would give me a little space to perform?"

"Wait a second," Mother Duck protested. "This is not what I had in mind."

But the damsel had already launched into song:

> "Do you have a friend who's feeling down?
> Who's cold and has a chill?
> If you need a cure to come around
> That's better than a pill
> Good song and dance then must be found
> And Damsel and Dragon will!"

Mother Duck looked from the performers to me, her gaze an odd mix of disbelief and nausea. "They do this sort of thing all the time, don't they?"

"Indeed," I answered, this time truthfully.

"Pardon us."

I looked down to see that we had been joined by Smarmy and his fellow dwarves, who had entered our group unnoticed, thanks to the nearby performance.

Smarmy wrung his hands as he looked up apologetically. "We thought we were coming to rescue someone—" He glanced apprehensively at the dancing dragon "—but maybe we should have stayed away."

I sympathized with the dwarf, for at that moment, Damsel and Dragon began another verse.

> "Do you know someone who's feeling low,
> Near the end of his life span?
> And they need a pick-me-up to go
> So they don't feel like an also-ran?
> They need song and dance that's fast, not slow
> And Damsel and Dragon can!"

"We came out of the woods for this?" Nasty complained.

"Pay no attention," Snooty admonished. " 'Tis naught but entertainment for the rabble."

Sickly coughed contemptuously.

"Hey!" the Brownie demanded. "Who are you calling *rabble?*"

"Not me!" Touchy insisted.

"Although he would have if he'd thought of it!" Nasty sneered.

Dumpy moaned in agreement.

"What's going on here?" Snarks demanded, stepping between Tap and the dwarves. "Did I hear someone criticizing the dancers?"

"Do you hear anyone *not* criticizing the dancers?" Nasty retorted.

"Oh, wow," Spacey agreed.

"They were making fun of us, too!" Tap interjected. "They called us rabble!" He stopped for an instant, so upset he could barely breathe. "They're making fun of Brownie Power!"

"Doom," Hendrek remarked as he pushed his great bulk amidst the throng. "Is someone here causing trouble?"

"I suppose you never cause trouble!" Touchy demanded. "I suppose you never criticize anybody!"

Tap and Hendrek both looked at Snarks.

"Well, it's different for me," the truth-telling demon replied hurriedly. "And look, a little constructive criticism never hurt anybody. So I get to call them awful once in a while. They're my companions, after all. They expect it of me!"

"Doom," Hendrek added. "It pays to be polite."

Tap nodded. "That's what Brownie Power's all about!"

Nasty looked to his fellows. "So that means we have to be polite to this rabble?"

Snarks stared grimly at the upstart drawf as Hendrek hefted his club and Tap did a few tentative dance steps.

"Doom," Hendrek remarked.

Brax stepped between the combatants. "Pardon me for butting in, but is anyone here in the market for a previously owned weapon?"

But just then, Damsel and Dragon launched into another verse:

"So if you know someone who's feeling bad,
    And you want to make them well,
    We've got an answer, so don't be sad,
    For soon they'll be feeling swell!
    Song and dance'll be the best time they ever had,
    And Damsel and Dragon shall!"

Guxx's sneezes redoubled as he rolled about in the dirt.

"Do you have the feeling this is getting out of hand?" Mother Duck inquired.

I did not answer her for fear that, if I agreed, she would again put us all under her spell.

"Perhaps this is too big a challenge for me, after all," she murmured, more to herself than to me. "Perhaps I'd be better restricting my fairy tales to golden geese and blind mice?"

Alea began an elaborate tap dance across Hubert's wings.

"If only I liked my name better," the old woman continued. "Having a name like Mother Duck sometimes causes one to lose confidence. But I've told you about that, haven't I?"

The Seven Other Dwarves and my companions in the quest glowered at each other.

"Oh, yeah?" the dwarves shouted.

"Doom," my companions replied.

The situation was getting tenser by the minute. But if I asked Mother Duck to intervene, she would control us all, robbing me of my free will!

"Mother Robin?" the old woman mused, then shook her head. "Entirely too singsong. How about Mother Bluebird?" She pursed her lips, then frowned. "Too much alliteration. Mother Red-Winged Blackbird?" She sighed. "Altogether too long. How would they fit in on my books? Oh, I know I shouldn't grouse—wait a minute, that's not bad at all." She looked at me in triumph. "Mother Grouse! Well, perhaps it's not perfect, but it certainly sounds better than Mother Duck, don't you think?"

"Indeed," I replied, mostly to keep the conversation going. Mother Duck seemed to handle chaos badly; it was also the only time she chose to talk to me. I had failed before in persuading her to join our cause. I wondered if there might be some other way I could turn this situation to my advantage.

Damsel and Dragon had slowed their dance to a shuffle.

"Tell me, Damsel," Hubert began.

"Yes, Dragon?" Alea answered.

"How do my fellow lizards build their homes?" the dragon asked.

"Oh, that's easy," Damsel chorused. "With Rep-Tiles!"

"But I understand you can really swing," Alea continued after the groans had subsided.

Hubert wiggled his posterior. "Sure can. But that's another tail altogether!"

The crowd reaction to that one was even worse.

"But enough of clever patter!" Hubert shouted over the din. "Now here's a number that really makes me want to shed my skin!"

"I think not!" Mother Duck exclaimed, raising both her hands. "No, this is too much. Total confusion is one thing. That I can handle. The way chaos constantly settles around the Eternal Apprentice is interesting, to say the least. Vaudeville humor, on the other hand—" She did not quite suppress a shudder. "I'd better put everyone back under my power before something else happens."

Jeffrey the Wolf waved his green cap at the old woman. "May I make a suggestion?"

Mother Duck sighed. "If you must."

"You worry about your fairy tales becoming too chaotic," Jeffrey added quickly. "Well, I have a solution to your problems." He thumped his chest for emphasis. "We talking wolves are fairy tale professionals! Just put me in your next story, and my tried and true enchanted tale experience will guarantee a classic!"

"Perhaps," the old woman said warily.

"You won't be sorry," Jeffrey promised.

"Mother Duck is never sorry. But you might be." She shook her head smartly, as if the contents needed to be slightly rearranged. "All right," she agreed wearily. "Heaven knows I've tried everything else."

She surveyed the whole group before her. "Now, everyone repeat after me: Once upon—"

The earth began to shake. We all backed away quickly as a crevice yawned in our midst. As usual, there was a cloud of dust, and when it cleared, we saw a table with five demons.

"We've got you now!" the gavel demon cried in triumph.

It was the Netherhells again.

THIRTEEN

"Guxx Unfufadoo, concernèd demon,
Asks you why you read quotations,
When you know Wuntvor's in danger;
Says you should get on with chapter!"

—The preceding was provided by
The Equal Time for Demons Act,
Vushta common law 77034
(recently repealed)

"This time," Mother Duck remarked, "you're in trouble."

All five demons caught sight of the angry old woman. All five demons blanched noticeably.

"Oh, dear!" the gavel demon exclaimed, attempting a smile. "We've made a mistake, haven't we?"

Mother Duck nodded. "Your last mistake."

"But we were sure this was Vushta!" the small, sickly demon at the end broke in.

"Maybe it's Vushta in disguise!" another committee member suggested.

"Yeah!" the demon in the flowered hat added. "Maybe

Mother Duck is in league with the wizards!"

"How dare you suggest such a thing?"

The demons all looked up, startled at Mother Duck's tone, for her voice had slid from heated anger to coldest rage.

"What do you think of me?" the old woman continued. "Consorting with wizards? From Vushta? What sort of a person do you think I am? Next, you'll have me taking tea with one of those grubby mages from the Western Kingdoms!"

The demons all began to talk at once.

"Oh no, Mother Duck."

"So sorry, Mother Duck."

"How could we have been so tactless as to make that mistake, Mother Duck?"

"You are demons," the old woman reminded them. "It is in your nature. What I cannot excuse, however, is your trespassing once again in the Eastern Kingdoms!"

"But the magic, Mother Duck—"

"It led us here, Mother Duck—"

"Oh, this is embarrassing," the gavel demon interjected. "Here we are, an elite corps of Netherhells mercenaries, and we can't even find Vushta. You'd think there'd be *some* magical activity going on there, wouldn't you? It is Vushta, after all. I mean, how else are they going to get those forbidden delights?"

"I am not interested in your problems," Mother Duck replied. "My only concern is that you are here again, interfering with the order of my fairy stories! If you cannot tell the difference between fairy magic and wizard magic, well—" She glanced meaningfully at Richard. "—I think it might be time to bake some bread."

"But Mother Duck, there was—"

"—Definite wizard magic, Mother Duck—."

"Please, Mother Duck, *any* demon can tell the difference between wizard magic and fairy tale magic!"

"What?" Mother Duck demanded. "Wizard magic? In my kingdom? Well, my demon committee, if what you say is true, you may have earned yourself a reprieve. Richard?"

"Oops!" the giant replied. "Didn't see that crevice there. I almost tripped. What do you wish, Mother Duck?"

"Look about my kingdom. Do you see anything strange?

Anything that looks out of the ordinary? Anything that might be a wizard?"

The giant shielded his eyes from the glare of the sun and looked east. "No, nothing there." He looked south. "No, nothing there, either."

He turned about to look north. "Oops. Darn it. I wish they wouldn't grow those trees so close together. But there's nothing out here, either."

At last, he turned west. "No, there's nothing this way, either. Well, there's that giant shoe, but that doesn't look anything like a wizard."

"Pardon!" Mother Duck peered up at the giant.

"It's a shoe," Richard repeated. "A very large shoe." He knelt down to touch his own. "Not as big as mine, maybe —"

He swung his shoe forward so that Mother Duck could get a better view. "Oops! Well, we probably didn't need that hill there, anyway. But it's still a pretty big shoe."

"Really?" Mother Duck stared thoughtfully at the committee. "I haven't made any giant shoes, at least not recently. Demons, you are correct. There is wizardry afoot!"

The five demons all fell to their knees.

"Thank you, Mother Duck!"

"Bless you, Mother Duck!"

"We knew you could recognize the truth, Mother Duck!"

At the moment, Mother Duck was content to watch the demons grovel, but I had to use the brief respite to think. My master had come to the Eastern Kingdoms to save me, but he had already been discovered by Mother Duck. Even worse, I had heard what she thought of western wizards. If she cornered the shoe, I knew my master was in real trouble! There had to be some way I could distract her and stop her from investigating.

"Indeed," I began, trying desperately to think of something that might delay her.

Mother Duck glanced down at me, a bit surprised. "Oh that's right! I haven't completed my controlling spell. Well, why don't you just sit here for a bit, like a good pawn, while I take care of this little difficulty?"

She turned back to the giant. "Richard, what say we visit this big new shoe?"

"Oops!" Richard replied.

Mother Duck scowled. "What's the matter now?"

The giant cowered at her tone. "The shoe is gone, Mother Duck. It is no longer on the western hill."

"A phantom shoe?" She rubbed her chin in thought. "How interesting. Perhaps we have an adversary worthy of Mother Duck. For I have a feeling we will be seeing that shoe again."

She turned back to the committee. "The information you've given me will be very useful. In fact, it will guarantee your continued existence. But make no mistakes! The Eastern Kingdoms are off limits to the Netherhells, now and forever. Come back again, and no excuse will be good enough!"

The five demons shouted assent as they pushed their table back toward the crevice.

"Yes, Mother Duck."

"Certainly, Mother Duck."

"Your mercy is astounding, Mother Duck."

"And what will happen to you if you come back?" She looked about at the rest of us, then smiled at the demons. "I don't really want to upset the others. I'll come over and describe it in detail."

"Must you, Mother Duck?"

"Can't we leave it up to our imagination, Mother Duck?"

"The last group you warned is still under the finest mental care the Netherhells can provide, Mother Duck."

But the old woman would not be stopped. She marched over to the committee and addressed them in low tones. An occasional word or two drifted my way on the breeze:

". . . pummel . . . dice . . . bake . . . julienne . . ."

"Pardon me," a voice said at my hip, "but can we talk?"

I looked down to see Smarmy wringing his hands.

"Indeed," I answered.

"Good," Smarmy replied, nodding toward his fellow dwarves, who had gathered in a semicircle around us. "Some of us, humble as we are, feel that it was only because you threw your lot in with us that you got captured by Mother Duck. We sort of got you into this and well, we'd like to get you out."

"Indeed?" I responded. "Do you have a plan?"

"Well, no," Smarmy admitted. "Not precisely. But, since it seems that Mother Duck is never going to use us again in her fairy tales, we have a lot of time on our hands. We'll come up with something."

"Yeah!" Nasty agreed. "Anything to get rid of those friends of yours!"

"That's correct," Snooty asserted. "The neighborhood used to be so nice, before you moved in."

Dumpy moaned. Sickly coughed. Noisy dropped something. So the dwarves were all in agreement.

"And I mean it this time!" Mother Duck called after the retreating demons. Calls of "Yes, Mother Duck!"—"Wouldn't have it any other way, Mother Duck!" and suchlike rose through the cloud of dust.

But I had other things to consider. The Seven Other Dwarves were going to help us escape. As were Norei, and His Brownieship, and the unicorn, and my master, the great wizard Ebenezum. Perhaps our situation was not as bleak as it seemed. With all these allies, our escape plans could not possibly fail. Could they?

But then there was Death. Somehow, the spectre had developed an obsession with me, and if I was ever left truly alone, whether I was under Mother Duck's control or not, I knew that Death would find me. Perhaps my master would find me, too, and rescue me again before the spectre could take me to his kingdom. That is, if my master could continue to elude Mother Duck's grasp. I sighed. Why did life have to be so complicated?

If only, I thought, I could keep some shred of self-control under Mother Duck's spell. I considered Norei's message, something about remembering three words: Happily ever after. I whispered them to myself now, as if they might be an antidote for what was to come.

"And now," Mother Duck remarked as she turned back to the rest of us, "what to do with all of you? For I think I was a trifle hasty a moment ago, when I tried to put you back into my spell. We need to consider a few things if we are going to create my masterpiece!"

She pointed at Hubert. "Firstly, I have insubordination to deal with. Perhaps the dragon did not recall certain prohibitions

I made about singing in my presence?"

"Oh, that?" Hubert did his best to laugh jovially. " 'Twas but the theater in my blood, bubbling over. You know what they say: Gotta sing, gotta dance?"

Mother Duck frowned at the dragon. "No one has 'gotta do' anything in my domain, at least anything that I do not decree. Therefore, as long as you are in my kingdoms, you will never speak again." She snapped her fingers three times.

"But it was only my acting exuberan—" Hubert's nostrils shook, smoke coming from his mouth and ears. "—urrgghh— but I mean—grahhh—couldn't you—unhhh." And the dragon was silent.

Mother Duck turned to Alea. "Be thankful that I need you to speak in your fairy tale role, or you would share your companion's fate. I mean, 'Damsel and Dragon shall'? There is only so much a professional storyteller can stand."

Alea looked up at Hubert, who kept opening and closing his mouth, all in the complete absence of sound.

"Yes, Mother Duck," she said nervously.

"Good," the old woman replied. "Then let that be a lesson to you all. Mother Duck must be obeyed!"

"Yes, Mother Duck," a number of my company replied quickly.

"Now, let's get on to specifics," she continued, satisfied with the response. "Mr. Wolf, you have volunteered your services?"

Jeffrey replied that he had.

"Well, that's fine, except— You don't want to do the one about the red riding hood, do you?" Mother Duck said with obvious distaste.

"Certainly not, Mother Duck," Jeffrey reassured her. "I have another story with even more drama, and an even bigger part for talking wolves."

The old woman nodded. "You never miss an opportunity. This should be interesting. In addition, I anticipate using all our characters this time—that might change your story a bit. And, as always, I will be supervising the action. I trust now that everybody understands their function?"

"Yes, Mother Duck," came the chorused reply.

"Good." She smiled. "That's what I like. One happy family. Jeffrey, if I might speak with you for a minute?"

"Excuse us, Mother Duck," the Seven Other Dwarves chorused in turn.

"Yes?" she answered, her expression halfway between annoyance and amusement.

"Pardon us for interrupting," Smarmy replied, "but did we hear you say that everyone will have a part?"

"Certainly." Mother Duck was all smiles again. "Oh dear, I have been ignoring you, my dwarves, what with all this new blood. Don't worry. You'll have a very important part."

"A very important part?" Snooty sniffed.

"Oh, wow," Spacey commented while Noisy cheered.

Mother Duck nodded at the wolf. "Jeffrey, if you don't mind?" The two of them retreated behind a stand of dead trees and conversed in hushed tones.

"Indeed," I whispered to Smarmy. "We must plan now. I fear our time is running out."

"Plan?" Smarmy chirped. "What do we need to plan? We've got a part!"

"A very important part!" Snooty added.

"You remember," I insisted. "What we were just talking about. My escape!"

"Escape?" Smarmy said the word as if he had never heard it before. "Oh, that. Well, I think escapes will simply have to wait. That is, unless they're part of the fairy story."

"A very important part!" Snooty elucidated.

"Indeed," I replied. Apparently, my escape plans had received a temporary setback. Now that the dwarves were included in Mother Duck's plans, they could think of nothing else.

"It will make a great beginning!" Mother Duck announced, shooing Jeffrey the Wolf back into our midst. She waved to the rest of us. "I will leave you a few moments of peace as I return to my hilltop observatory."

This time, Mother Duck marched off alone.

Jeffrey wore a big, wolfish grin as he walked toward us.

"This is going to be great," he assured us. "I tell you, we're going to see talking wolves like they've never been seen before!"

"Tell me," Brax inquired. "Have you ever considered a future selling used weapons? Franchises are available."

But I had no time for idle chatter. The fairy story would once again begin in earnest. I repeated the words Norei had given me, hoping against hope that they held some power:

"Happily ever after. Happily ever after. Once upon a time."

Everyone said that last sentence in unison with me.

FOURTEEN

Fairy tales can come true, it can happen to you, if you're stuck in Mother Duck's kingdom.

—Some Notes on Apprenticeship,
by Wuntvor, Apprentice to Ebenezum,
greatest wizard in the Western Kingdoms
(a work in progress)

Once upon a time there was a lad named Wuntvor, who had two good friends. One of the friends was large, both in height and width, and always carried an equally large club. The other friend, however, was just plain small, and tended to talk a lot about shoes. Still, the three of them got along famously, except for an argument here and there.

One day, Wuntvor remarked: "I heard there is a wolf skulking about the neighborhood."

"Doom," his large friend, whose name was Hendrek, replied. "You worry too much about these things."

"That's right!" the small fellow, who was known as Tap, chimed in. "Why worry about wolves when you can talk about shoes!"

Wuntvor thought the two of them were probably right. It was such a fine, sunny day, after all, and Tap could speak for hours about the intricacies of eyelet placement.

"Still," the lad said to the others, "you can't be too careful about these sorts of things. It is best to take precautions."

The other two laughed at his serious nature on such a sunny day, and went on to talk of other things. But little did any of them know that they were being watched at that very moment by the very wolf Wuntvor had mentioned!

Yum-yum, thought the wolf, whose name was Jeffrey. What tasty morsels these three would make. True, the little fellow would serve as not much more than an appetizer, but the enormous one could feed him for a week. And as for the young lad, well the wolf thought he just might be the right age and tenderness to make the most wonderful meal imaginable. Perhaps sauteed would be best, the wolf thought. But he had to be careful, for if he became too excited by the thought of his impending dinners he might reveal himself prematurely, and thus waste that all important element of surprise.

"Well," Wuntvor said at last, "it certainly has been pleasant whiling away an hour with the two of you, but I think it's time we got back to work."

"Doom," Hendrek agreed.

"Watch out for skulking wolves!" Tap cried over his shoulder with a laugh.

And then Wuntvor's two friends left and went their separate ways, for all three were in the construction business, and by odd coincidence, all of them were working on new homes for themselves.

Ah, thought the wolf. This is better than ever. Divide and conquer is always the best strategy. I shall pick them off one by one, and have enough tasty morsels to last me for weeks.

But where to start? The wolf frowned for a moment, but the answer was obvious. You always ate the appetizer before the main course. With that in mind, the hungry wolf skulked after the little fellow.

Jeffrey soon came to the edge of a clearing. He carefully hid in the bushes and watched the little fellow for a moment as Tap casually put the finishing touches on his house.

"I think the big boot should go here," Tap said to himself, placing an enormous brown boot at the peak of the roof. "And I can use these ten pairs of sandals as a walkway."

The wolf squinted to get a better look at the little fellow's handiwork, for the house he was building was different from any Jeffrey had ever seen. To call the structure ramshackle would be kind, for the house seemed to be made from hundreds or even thousands of small brown and black objects with all sorts of tones and textures. It took the wolf a long moment to determine the building material, for it was too dark to be mud, and too smooth to be brick.

And then he realized that the house was made entirely out of shoes.

Jeffrey the wolf was taken aback for a moment or two. Shoes? How could you make a house out of shoes? Not very well, was the only answer he could come up with. But then, the little fellow's badly built house fit right in with the hungry wolf's dining plans, for, when Jeffrey confronted Tap, the small one would have no safe place to go to.

The wolf skulked silently from his hiding place.

"Oh, a boot goes here," Tap sang to himself, "a slipper there, boot here, slipper there, shoes shoes everywhere—Who are you?"

Tap had seen the wolf! Jeffrey, however, put on his very best smile and stood up somewhat straighter than his skulking position.

"Hello, neighbor!" Jeffrey said cordially. "I just thought I'd drop by to admire this house you're building."

The little fellow beamed at that. "Yes, it is a fine house, is it not? Built of the finest shoe leather available."

"No doubt," the wolf replied, but he looked at Tap and not the house. Yes, he was quite sure of it now. He would be able to swallow the little fellow in a single gulp, perhaps after dipping him in a suitable sauce. Now, if only Tap did not move for another moment.

"What are you doing?" Tap demanded.

"Why, looking at your fine house," the wolf replied innocently.

"You were not!" the wee one insisted. "You were skulking!

My friend Wuntvor warned me about creatures who skulk! And you're a wolf besides!"

And with that, Tap ran inside the house and slammed the door.

Jeffrey chuckled to himself. He was not upset in the least. In fact, the wolf always loved this part best of all. He removed his cap, cleared his throat, and said in a loud voice:

"You should let me in and I'll know what to do!"

But Tap replied:

"Not by the laces of my shoesy-shoo-shoes!"

Jeffrey grinned even wider, and added:

"Then I'll huff and I'll puff and I'll bloooow your house down!"

The wolf took a very deep breath, inhaling for fully half a minute. Then, with lungs bursting, he positioned his snout for the very best velocity and trajectory, and blew. The ensuing gale easily destroyed Tap's house of shoes.

"Buckles and laces!" the little fellow exclaimed. "What have you done?"

Jeffrey's grin was so wide now that it showed every one of his long, pointed teeth. "Just gotten a little obstacle out of the way, so that we can get down to the serious business of dinner-time!"

"Oh, no you don't!" And the little fellow began to dance. And the fallen shoes around him began to dance as well, leaping higher and higher into the air. And closer and closer to the wolf, Jeffrey noticed in alarm. He backed away, but the shoes were faster. They jumped all about him, raining down on him in a merciless mass of shoe leather. The wolf fell to the ground, covering his head as best he could.

It seemed like hours before the footwear stopped moving. Jeffrey groaned as he climbed out of the pile of shoes. Something, it seemed, had gone wrong. He couldn't remember the story going this way. He moved a particularly nasty mound of boots away from his face, gasping for air. But he forgot to breathe, for the first thing he saw above the pile was another shoe, far bigger than all the rest, big enough even for a man or a wolf to hide inside.

"Indeed," the shoe remarked.

Jeffrey fell backward in alarm, slipping down again into the loose jumble of footwear. He struggled back to the surface quickly, but when he once again broke free of the sea of soles and heels, the giant shoe was gone.

It must have been some sort of hallucination, Jeffrey rationalized. It was all perfectly explainable. It was some sort of reaction to being attacked by so much footwear. After all, what other reason would there be for a shoe of that size to even exist? The wolf decided he was better off not even thinking about it.

But the little fellow had escaped as well. And the wolf realized, now that he had started thinking about food, that he was ravenously hungry. Whose house should he blow down next? With an appetite like his, there was really no choice.

"Once upon a time," the wolf whispered, and went about his work.

If anything, Jeffrey the Wolf was even hungrier now. It was making him lose his judgment. He had startled a unicorn just beyond the house he sought, and the wolf hadn't even thought to chase it. But the unicorn no longer mattered, for Jeffrey had at last located the object of his desire, a meal large enough to sate even his enormous appetite.

"Doom doom," Hendrek hummed tunelessly as he built a wall out of what seemed to be random objects, although many of them were long and shiny. "Doom-de-doom-doom-doom."

It was then that the wolf realized that Hendrek was not alone. Well, Jeffrey thought, all well and good, for every diet needs a little variety. Or at least he thought that until he got a good look at the assistant, who was busy handing Hendrek his building materials. The other fellow was short and squat, and sort of an unhealthy grayish-green in color, besides which he had the most horrendous taste in clothes imaginable, wearing some sort of orange and purple checked coat. Perhaps, the ravenous beast considered, the large fellow would be more than enough for dinner. After all, even a wolf as hungry as Jeffrey had some standards.

The wolf left the concealing bushes to get closer to the object of his hunger.

"Doom," Hendrek noted. "We have a visitor."

His assistant looked up. "Oh, you mean that guy skulking over there?"

Jeffrey chose to ignore that remark, instead standing up straight and doffing his cap.

"And a good day to you, too, neighbors," he greeted them cheerily. "What a fine house you are building!"

"Doom," Hendrek agreed.

"Made out of the finest previously-owned materials available," the incredibly ugly assistant added. "My previously owned materials."

"Doom," Hendrek replied, lifting an imposing looking warclub.

"Of course, most certainly!" Brax added hurriedly. "We have an arrangement."

"Doom." Hendrek nodded. "The arrangement is he lends me his previously owned materials, or I use Headbasher."

The wolf nodded pleasantly, although he was not really listening. Instead, he wondered what would be just the right method of attack to quickly subdue this large and certainly tasty Hendrek. Perhaps, Jeffrey decided at last, if he strolled around a bit behind him. He pictured the large fellow coated with a thin honey glaze.

"There he goes," the assistant remarked, "skulking again."

"Doom," the large fellow added, "he also appears to be a wolf."

"Are you going to hold something as small as that against me?" Jeffrey tried to smile innocently.

"You know, Hendy baby," the assistant replied as he looked closely at the wolf's long and pointed teeth, "perhaps it's time we went and worked on the interior of the house, with the front door securely closed and locked?"

"Doom," Hendrek agreed.

The two of them retreated inside. But all the wolf did was smile even more, for they had gotten to his favorite part of the story once again. He took a deep breath and called out:

"Come on and let me into your front room!"

But Hendrek boomed back:

"Not by the hair of my doom-de-doom-doom!"

Jeffrey chuckled. Now was the moment for the really good

part. And this time, there weren't any of those nasty shoes around here to ruin it for him.

He took a bigger breath: "Then I'll huff and I'll puff and I'll bloooooow your house down!" And he took the biggest breath he possibly could, feeling as though his lungs would burst right through his hairy chest. He quickly positioned his snout once again for maximum effect, and blew.

Hendrek's house didn't stand a chance. It came apart with a clatter. Hundreds of shiny things flew into the air.

And then they started to fall down. Jeffrey looked up in the sky and realized with a horrible sickening certainty exactly what Hendrek had built his house with. For spread overhead, but descending quickly, were spears and arrows and knives and scimitars and broadswords, and any number of other long, sharp and pointy things.

And they all seemed to be falling toward Jeffrey.

The previously owned objects Hendrek had built his house with were all weapons. What sort of person built a house out of weapons? By now, Jeffrey was quite certain this was not the way the story was supposed to go. But he was even more certain that if he stood his ground he would be skewered at least a dozen times.

Jeffrey ran back into the woods with a howl. The wolf knew he would have to look elsewhere for dinner. But it would be the tenderest dinner of all.

Wuntvor worked diligently on his sturdy, new brick house. As nice as it was to discuss shoes and the issues of the day with his two good friends, it was even nicer to be alone for a change.

But wasn't the day growing suddenly cold? Perhaps it was only that chill wind that had sprung up so suddenly. It was an amazingly ferocious breeze, stripping the leaves from the surrounding trees. Wuntvor was glad he would soon have a nice, warm house to protect him from the weather. And then he heard another sound, a dry, hollow chuckle, as cold in its way as the wind that had preceded it. Wuntvor looked up. He thought he saw a dark figure walking between the trees.

Was someone coming?

FIFTEEN

There is another saying among those mages I am always talking about: "If a man can stand tall and proud, he will not be afraid." And perhaps there is some truth in this statement, for if a man can stand tall and proud, with a good weapon or two in his hands, a trusted banishment spell upon his lips, and his back against the wall, then his fear might diminish considerably. Even better is the scenario where he has two or three hundred trusted allies at his side, a nearby trap door for hasty escapes, and no enemy approaching for miles around. It gets better still when you add a tidy sum stashed away in a handy retirement account, the love of a good woman and a hiding place that no one else has discovered in hundreds of years. Under such circumstances, fear could conceivably be controlled. But don't count on it.

—The Teachings of Ebenezum, VOLUME LV

Wuntvor was suddenly afraid. There was something about this sort of weather, something about that mysterious figure, that he should remember. Everything around him seemed like ice.

Even his clothes were cold against his body.

Somebody coughed.

Wuntvor jumped. There was a rustling in the bushes.

"Oh, wow," another voice said.

"Aren't you going to say hello?" yet another voice demanded. "It's getting cold out here!"

"Beg pardon?" Wuntvor replied as eight fairly short men emerged from the shrubbery. He looked up as a distant scream echoed eerily through the forest, as if a hundred lost souls cried their death agonies. But then the day warmed again as suddenly as it had cooled, and the late afternoon sun once more shone through the treetops.

"Weird weather patterns you have around here," one of the short fellows muttered as he wrung his hands. "But that's not why we're here."

"Indeed?" Wuntvor replied, somewhat dubiously. "Have we met?"

"Must he always say that?" one of the dwarves complained.

"Don't mind Touchy, there," the hand-wringer quickly added. "You would recall us, if you were not under one of Mother Duck's spells."

"Indeed?" Wuntvor wasn't really trying to comprehend what these short people were talking about. There was something about the cold wind and the mysterious figure which somehow seemed much more important.

"I'm sorry," he added at last. "I don't remember."

"Of course not!" the hand-wringer agreed with him jovially. "You're in a fairy tale. The very tale in which we have been promised a major role!"

"This doesn't seem very major to me!" one of the others sniffed.

"Of course not, Snooty," the hand-wringer answered. "Our major role hasn't started yet. This is more of a cameo appearance." He turned back to Wuntvor. "But, we came to admire your new home!" He added in a lower voice: "I'd introduce everybody, but what's the use? The way things have been going lately, Mother Duck will have to start this whole thing over again in a minute, anyway." He continued in his louder, more forceful conversational style: "My this certainly looks like a sturdy horse. We were awfully glad to get the opportunity to see it!" For some reason, the short fellow glanced at his wrist. "Look how late it's gotten to be! Well, we have to run!"

The speaker waved as he and his fellows turned to go.

"That's it?" Wuntvor asked. "That's all you came here to tell me?"

"Why, of course!" the hand-wringing fellow called back over his shoulder. "Still, if our appearance here serves to remind Mother Duck that we're still around, eager to begin our part in this drama, that couldn't hurt, either."

"Wait a minute!" Wuntvor called, desperation rising in his voice. For he had suddenly remembered that that mysterious figure wanted to capture him, but could only do so if he was all alone.

"What is it this time?" one of the others barked.

"Um—," Wuntvor fumbled, trying to think fast. "Wouldn't you like to see the inside of my house?"

"If it's as boring as the outside, no way!" the same fellow added. "It's enough that we have to go along with Smarmy's publicity ideas here—"

"But we all agreed—," the hand-wringer interrupted.

"Only so that we didn't have to put up with your whining—"

"Oh, wow."

Somebody moaned. Somebody else coughed. A third somebody dropped something, very loudly.

"Oh, dear," the hand-wringer said at last. "Well, if it's that way, I'm afraid our humble selves really must be going."

Then they were still leaving? Wuntvor fought a panic that seemed to sweep over him from nowhere. How could he make them understand?

"But I'm all alone!" he wailed.

The brashest of the fellows snickered. "Sure you're all alone, except for that guy skulking over there in the bushes!"

The wolf stepped out from his hiding place. "Skulking? Me? Never. I just feel it is impolite to interrupt."

All eight of the short fellows laughed as they walked away.

"Nevermind them," the wolf scoffed. "I've come to look at your fine new home."

Nevermind them? Wuntvor didn't even understand them. He

had no idea why those eight short fellows had shown up. "Once upon a time," he muttered under his breath, turning his attention to the furry fellow with the green cap, who seemed quite a bit closer than the last time Wuntvor had looked. At this distance, he couldn't help but notice the size of the beast's incisors.

"Is something the matter?" the wolf inquired smoothly.

"Um—," Wuntvor began, trying to phrase his observation as politely as possible. "My, what big teeth you have."

The wolf shook his head peremptorily. "No, I'm sorry, that's another fairy tale altogether."

The lad looked down at the ground, trying to think of a suitable apology. But when he looked up again, the beast was almost on top of him.

The wolf licked his chops. "Speaking of appearances, you'd look particularly good in a light cream sauce." The wolf wiggled its shaggy eyebrows. "But perhaps others have told you that."

Wuntvor frowned. Come to think of it, somebody or other *had* told him that once, somewhere or other. Or at least Wuntvor thought they had. Didn't he? But what did it all mean?

"Doom," came a deep, booming voice from the bushes.

"You'd better watch out," a much smaller and higher voice added. "Or it'll be time for Brownie Power!"

The wolf frowned. This was *definitely* not the way this story was supposed to go. After all he'd promised Mother Duck, his fairy tale was getting out of hand as well.

"That's right!" Wuntvor declared, as if a veil had been lifted from his eyes. "That's what you were doing when you snuck up on me. You were skulking!" He pointed at the beast's open mouth. "That must mean that you're the wolf!"

"Doom!" Hendrek exclaimed as he charged from the bushes, his warclub high above his head. Tap cheered from where he clung to the large fellow's shoulder.

"Hey!" the wolf protested, covering his head. "Give a guy a break. I'm only trying to make a living!"

"Doom!" Hendrek replied, grabbing Wuntvor by his shirt. "Into the house!"

And the three friends ran inside, slamming the very heavy oak door behind them.

Jeffrey uncovered his head and stared at the thick door. This fairy tale had gotten so far off course that even he could barely recognize it. He decided not to even try the next part, with the huffing and puffing. The wolf was a realist, after all. He knew all about his luck with brick houses.

But there were other ways of getting food. The wolf laughed ruefully at the closed doors. All right, my dinner delicacies, he thought. If that's the way you want it, that's the way it's going to be.

They had tricked him with houses made of shoes and weapons. Well, there was more than one way to end a fairy tale. He'd show them that a wolf could improvise as well!

And with that, the wolf skulked back into the forest.

In the meantime, the three friends huddled within Wuntvor's brick house.

"Doom," Hendrek remarked. "Isn't it a little dark in here?"

"Yeah!" Tap added. "The only light's coming from that little hole overhead!"

"Indeed." Wuntvor looked up at the small portal that still showed the early evening sky. "That is the only part of my house that I haven't finished."

"Doom," Hendrek commented. "Don't you think you should have put in windows?"

Wuntvor considered, then shook his head, a motion that was almost lost in the gathering gloom. "Windows wouldn't have been wolfproof. I had a singleness of purpose when I built this house. Still, this place isn't much good for anything but hiding, is it?"

They opened the door and peered out. The sun had sunk far below the trees, and deep shadows stretched across Wuntvor's lawn, as if the night had already claimed the ground and was working on the sky. It was difficult to see anything in the gathering dusk, but they all heard a great crashing and tearing that was coming closer.

"Doom," Hendrek whispered. "What could that be?"

"Indeed," Wuntvor added. "It doesn't sound like a wolf."

Tap jumped boldly from Hendrek's shoulder. "I am small and will be difficult to see in the shadows. I will go investigate."

And before either of his friends could protest, he was gone.

The crashing grew louder still, and was accompanied by bestial laughter.

"Tap?" Wuntvor called softly into the night. "Can you see

anything? Is there something we should do?"

The little fellow's answer was to run back inside and hide behind the lad's leg.

"Close the door!" Tap yelled. "Close the door!"

"But what did you see?" Wuntvor inquired.

"Big . . ." the little fellow gasped. "Scaly . . . Fire-breathing . . ."

"Doom," Hendrek rumbled. "The wolf has brought a dragon."

"A dragon?" Wuntvor wondered. "What could he do—"

But his conjecture was cut short by the wolf's call:

"Open your door or I'll vent my frustration!"

"Indeed?" Wuntvor whispered to the others. "Maybe this isn't as bad as we think. Maybe there's some way we can talk this out." He called back to the wolf:

"Is this request open to negotiation?"

The wolf could barely restrain his laughter as he yelled: "Then we'll huff and we'll puff and we'll blllooooooowww your house down!"

"Duck!" Wuntvor called as a great roaring sound came from without.

Wuntvor and the others fell to the earthen floor, covering their heads to protect them from flying bricks. But the house was so well put together that the dragon's breath picked it up as a single piece and sent it soaring into the night sky.

Wuntvor stood, looking out at the clearing still lit by dragon fire. The wolf smiled and licked his chops.

"This will all be so much simpler if you just stand there," the beast remarked, stepping forward. "And don't worry at all. The light cream sauce is quite tasty."

"Doom." Hendrek shifted his warclub from hand to hand.

"Buckles and laces!" Tap tried out some tentative dance steps.

"I'll get around to both of you later," the wolf replied, advancing on the lad.

Wuntvor felt helpless. He knew his friends would do the best they could to protect him. Still, he would feel much better if he had some way to protect himself, a weapon with which to smite the beast.

"That's a good meal," the wolf consoled. "It'll all be over

in a few seconds. I'm a very speedy eater."

"Oh, no you don't!" shouted a magnificently modulated voice from the other side of the clearing.

"What are you doing?" another voice complained. "Where are you taking me?"

Wuntvor looked in the direction of the commotion. There stood a magnificent beast, the color of moonlight, with a pale horn in the middle of its forehead. And in its mouth, it held a shining sword.

"So are you going to let me down, or what?" the sword whined.

"I am returning you to your rightful owner," the unicorn replied haughtily, somehow enunciating perfectly even with a sword in its mouth. It laid the sword at Wuntvor's feet, then looked up at the lad with its large, soulful eyes.

"I hope that you will be properly grateful," the beauteous beast whispered.

"Indeed," Wuntvor replied. "Perhaps we can discuss it some time, when we are not in the midst of a crisis." He knelt down and picked up the sword.

"Sure, you guys can talk!" Cuthbert continued. "Don't even give a thought to the trusty weapon who just spent half an hour stuck in that beast's mouth. I mean, my entire blade is covered with unicorn saliva! Yuck!"

"There is no more beautiful saliva upon the face of the earth," the unicorn retorted, shaking its moonlit mane to breathtaking effect.

"I am sure there is not," Wuntvor agreed, "but if you'll excuse me, I have a wolf to fend off."

"Oh, so that's the way it is, huh?" The wolf's teeth set in a grim smile. "Well, you may have a unicorn on your side, not to mention a talking sword and a big fellow with a club and a little fellow who does funny things with shoes. But I have a dragon!" He looked back at the imposing fire lizard. "Isn't that right?"

The dragon stared back at him silently.

"Hey!" the wolf insisted. "I thought we had a deal!" He took a step toward the dragon.

The dragon took a step away.

"Oh, no you don't!" the wolf yelled. "An arrangement is an arrangement!" The wolf took two steps forward.

The dragon took two steps away. And, being as the dragon was perhaps twenty times the size of the wolf, the giant lizard's steps were perhaps twenty times that of the green-hatted beast. In fact, the dragon had already backed completely out of the clearing.

"Is that so?" The wolf shook both his forepaws at the distant reptile. "I'll show you what I do to welchers!" He ran toward the dragon. The dragon retreated even more quickly. In a matter of seconds, both were out of sight.

There were twin explosions, one to either side of Wuntvor. The lad jumped back, startled. To his left was a little man, about the same size as Tap, although the newcomer seemed to be wearing a leather crown. And to his right was a huge shoe.

"Good," the shoe remarked. "Now we can talk."

SIXTEEN

There is an explanation for everything. It is a pity that many of those explanations make no sense.

—The Teachings of Ebenezum, VOLUME LXIX

I blinked. It was my master Ebenezum, come to rescue me once again.

"Indeed," he said. I realized I was staring.

"It must be very disconcerting for you," my master inside the shoe continued, "popping in and out of fairy tales like this."

"Um—," I replied. "Indeed."

"Well," my master continued, "I believe our dragon distraction has given us a few minutes. But we must talk quickly."

I nodded, trying to blink away the cobwebs that filled my brain.

Ebenezum explained: "Ever since Norei learned you were a prisoner of Mother Duck, we have been working together to set you free. And when His Brownieship was nice enough to reconstruct this magic shoe, I was able to enter the fray."

"That's Brownie Power for you!" His Brownieship added.

"I've been telling them that all along!" Tap replied.

His Brownieship looked balefully at his subordinate. "I don't think you should be talking to anybody."

Tap paled. "Heel sorting!" he whispered.

"Indeed," Ebenezum continued. "Before I came here, I was able through the protective powers of this shoe to study some of the learned books in Vushta concerning the Eastern Kingdoms. We have come up with some very important facts."

"Bent buckle straightening!" Tap moaned.

"Firstly, whenever you say 'Once—' " Ebenezum stopped himself abruptly. He cleared his throat and began again. "Well, you know those four words that always start the tales, and put you under Mother Duck's spell. There are three other words that end them, and close the loop, so that the fairy tale becomes fixed, with exactly the right ending."

"Happily ever after," Wuntvor whispered.

"Precisely," the wizard replied. "We are now concocting a scheme by which you, as the tale's primary participant, say exactly those words at exactly the right time." My master chuckled. "If we can plan this correctly, Wuntvor, this is your last fairy tale."

"Indeed?" I replied, fresh hope filling my heart. I knew my master would not let me down!

"Truly," he continued. "All we had to do was somehow find a way to inform you of our plan. Unfortunately, when I first arrived, we had to deal instantly with Death. And since that occasion, I have been trying to keep a low profile. If Mother Duck discovers our plot too soon, we will fail. I have tried instead to feed you hints, snuck into the corners of the fairy story. But that method has not been fast enough."

"So we had to create a diversion!" His Brownieship explained. Tap wouldn't look him in the eye.

"Indeed," the wizard resumed. "We needed to get the wolf out of the way. What you were just in, you realize, was *his* fairy story. Frustrated at the lack of control she has had over her own tales, Mother Duck gave the wolf a chance to see if he could do any better. Once we found out about this, we knew it was our chance. Anyway, it was His Brownieship's idea to add the dragon and the unicorn as a bit of a distraction. Now all we have to do is hope Mother Duck watches the wolf for a moment so we can talk."

There was one question he had not answered. I could not help myself—I had to ask it!

"But master!" I cried. "What of Norei?"

"Norei cannot be here. She is using her powers to watch Mother Duck, to make sure we are not discovered. She was also the one to see the opportunity in the wolf's tale."

My master paused. I imagined him stroking his long white beard deep within his shoe. "In addition, she is one of the few people with magical abilities to still escape my malady. She needs to stay hidden, safe from Mother Duck's power, until we finally put our plan into effect. Listen carefully, Wuntvor, for when we give you a prearranged signal, you must shout out those words."

"Happily ever after," I repeated once again.

"They have a satisfying ring to them, don't they?" His Brownieship smiled. "Sort of like Brownie Magic!"

Tap could hold it in no longer. "B-but my King of Sole!" he stuttered. "Won't you listen to me? I have always been true to Brownie Magic!"

His leader looked condescendingly down his royal nose. "Like those seven Brownie wishes?"

"But your smallness, once you hear—" Tap paused, as if struggling to pick the right words. "Once you—Once upon a time." His voice fell to a monotone, his eyes free of expression.

His Brownieship scowled. "The weak-willed always go first."

"She is reasserting control!" the wizard exclaimed. "Quickly, Wuntvor! There is one more thing I must tell you."

"Once upon—," His Brownieship began. He clapped his tiny hands over his mouth. I felt the pressure, too; those four words pounding in my brain, welling upon my lips. I had the feeling that speaking those words was as important as life itself. But I must fight it! I looked quickly to my companions, and saw from their distress that, now that my master had explained the true nature of the magic, they were battling the spell as well.

"We must go!" the wizard called. And both Ebenezum and His Brownieship disappeared in twin puffs of smoke.

"But master?" I asked the empty air. "What else must I know?"

"Doom," Hendrek remarked. "Ebenezum is resourceful. I

am sure he will find some way to tell us."

But the Brownie was back in the fairy tale trance; a spell that any of the rest of us could fall victim to at any moment. That meant that Mother Duck's eyes and ears were with us as well. How could my master give us his message without her finding out?

I looked up in the sky. Something had blotted out the moon. I heard the sound of great wings, descending rapidly. Even in the darkness, I knew it had to be Hubert.

"Here we are again!" Alea's voice called from Hubert's back. "It's the duo who will pull you through-o, the act of acts with all the facts!"

"The pair so slick that they'll make you sick!" another, incredibly annoying voice called from the edge of the clearing. I squinted into the darkness. Anyone wearing that many robes had to be Snarks.

"I had to come and see what would make this much noise," the demon explained. "Guxx is out there somewhere looking for his drummer. I imagine they will both be along presently."

"Indeed," I replied, careful to choose only the safest words possible. Now that I was searching for it, I could feel a subtle pressure within my skull, something there that wanted me to forget, perhaps to sleep. It was a powerful magic that I would have to fight if I wished to discover the rest of my master's message.

"Once upon a time," Tap interjected.

"Doom," Hendrek said, his brow furrowed as he studied me critically. "Then you feel it, too?"

I nodded. "I wish there was some way my master could hurry."

"Oh," Alea said brightly as she jumped from the dragon's back. "That's why we're here. Hubert knows!"

"Indeed?" Hubert knew the final secret my master wished to impart to me? But then I realized the terrible irony of the situation. "He cannot speak! How can he tell us?"

"Simple enough," the damsel reassured us. "It will be difficult, but Hubert can do it. He will have to utilize an ancient art among his kind: Dragon charades!"

Alea quickly outlined the rules of this ancient reptilian art as Hubert silently prepared himself. It seemed that the dragon would pantomime Ebenezum's secret, and those of us assembled here would have to guess the dragon's meaning. When one of us got it right, Hubert would nod and point, and the truth would be revealed to us.

"Simple enough," I announced. "Shall we begin?"

The dragon nodded, blowing controlled bursts of flame to better illuminate his actions.

Alea ran over to join the rest of us.

The dragon snapped his mouth open and shut repeatedly.

"It's a saying!" Alea exclaimed. "That's what Hubert's telling us. The wizard's message is a saying."

So Ebenezum had tried to tell me some ancient truth?

"What kind of saying?" I asked Alea.

"Once upon a time," Tap suggested.

"Watch Hubert and find out," she replied. "What a performer!"

I turned my attention back to the dragon.

"What's the saying about?" I called.

The dragon pointed downward. "The ground?" He shook his head. "The Netherhells?" His headshaking redoubled. I realized then that he was actually pointing to his lower extremities.

"Your feet?" I queried.

The dragon shrugged, then nodded. What did that mean—maybe? The dragon lifted one foot, then bent over so that he held both his forepaws just below his toes. With great care, he pulled the forepaws back toward his heel.

"Doom," Hendrek conjectured. "He is putting something over his foot."

"Like a shoe?" I asked.

The dragon nodded, thumping his tail enthusiastically.

"So the saying is about a shoe?"

The dragon nodded again.

"Doom," Hendrek added. "We have an expert about shoes."

"Once upon a time," Tap replied.

"Yes, but the Brownie is under Mother Duck's spell," I reminded the warrior. "She has taken over his mind."

"Doom," Hendrek acknowledged. "Perhaps I can remedy that."

"Once upon a time," Tap replied.

The warrior lifted his great warclub Headbasher, cursed to steal the memories of men, and gently bopped Tap on the noggin.

"Once upon an—urk!" Tap exclaimed. "Hey, watch out with that thing! We Brownies crush pretty easily."

"Indeed!" I cheered. "You have broken Mother Duck's spell."

"Doom," Hendrek agreed.

"Spell? I was under Mother Duck's spell?" Tap paled. "Where's His Brownieship?"

I told Tap that his leader had to flee to escape Mother Duck. I also told the Brownie that there might be a way he could redeem himself. All he had to do was figure out the famous saying about shoes that Hubert was trying to give us via sign language.

"Shoes?" Tap laughed. " 'Twill take but a moment for an expert like myself. Show me this pantomiming dragon!"

Hubert waved, then went back through the motions of putting on the shoe.

"Simplicity itself!" the Brownie exclaimed. "The saying is: A shoe in the hand is worth two in the bush."

The dragon shook his head.

"No?" Tap replied, clearly astonished that he had been incorrect. "Then it must be 'A rolling shoe gathers no laces!'—right?"

Hubert shook his head again, resorting once more to the putting-on-the-shoe pantomime.

"Too many Brownies spoil the shoe?" Tap tried again. "It just has to be!"

The dragon shook his head one more time as he tucked his foot into the imaginary footwear.

But that was it, I thought. Could it be?

"If the shoe fits, wear it!" I called.

Hubert nodded and pointed.

"If the shoe fits, wear it?" The Brownie scratched his tiny head. "I've never heard of that one. Doesn't seem to have much pizzazz, does it?"

Well, it might not have much "pizzazz," as the Brownie put

it, but since it came from my master, I was sure that it was fraught with meaning. But what could that meaning be?

"Aha!" yet another voice called from the edge of the clearing. "There you are!"

The speaker approached Hubert's flickering nose light. It was the wolf.

"Thought better of running away from me, did you?" the wolf asked superiorly. "Well, I'm glad we're back where we can get something done. On with the story!"

"No! No! No! No! No! No! No!" Mother Duck ran rapidly down the hill.

"What do you mean, no?" Jeffrey the Wolf complained as the old woman burst into our midst. "I was so close."

"Close to total chaos, you mean?" Mother Duck retorted angrily. "I knew I should never have listened to you."

"But I've almost gotten to the best part!" Jeffrey objected. "Where I get to eat everybody!" He turned to the dragon. "Now, if you'll just quick-fry all these characters over here—"

"Oh, no, you don't!" Mother Duck interrupted. "I'm taking back my fairy tale, as of now!"

She smiled at the assemblage.

"Once upon a time," we all said as one.

SEVENTEEN

"Everybody needs their rest."
— Yet another quote attributed to Ebenezum,
greatest wizard in the Western Kingdoms,
when he was once again discovered upon
the royal bed and in the arms of the
obviously enthusiastic Queen Vivazia
by her husband, King Snerdlot the
Vengeful. Luckily for the wizard, the
king was exhausted by endless hours of
Ebenezum-hunting in the hidden corridors
of the castle, and so was easily fooled
by the mage's temporary confusion spell,
which somehow got Snerdlot thinking that
he had wandered by mistake into the
wrong castle altogether, thus allowing
the wizard to escape back into the
hidden corridors during
the king's lengthy apology.

Once upon a time there was a handsome prince named Wuntvor,
who lived far out in the woods with his good friends, the Seven

Other Dwarves. Now the Seven Other Dwarves warned
Wuntvor to beware of strangers, for it was rumored—

No, no, no. That didn't sound at all right. Perhaps if he
rephrased it.

Once upon a time there was a very confused young man
named Wuntvor, who could have sworn there was something
that he was supposed to remember. And he also could have
sworn he should have known all the various people and beasts
that surrounded him in the clearing.

"Once upon a time," everyone said in unison, including
Wuntvor. But why? Wuntvor had no idea. Wasn't he supposed
to say something else instead?

"Are you just going to let me drag on the floor all day?" a
voice complained from just below his right wrist.

Wuntvor lifted the object he held in his right hand. It was
a sword.

"Much better!" the sword remarked.

"A talking sword?" Wuntvor almost dropped the weapon in
surprise.

"Oh, we're not going to start this again!" the sword admonished. "You're in another one of Mother Duck's fairy tales,
where she wipes out everyone's memory so that you can be
empty pawns that she can use at her whim. But you're nothing
of the sort." The sword sighed. "I suppose I'm going to have
to go through this whole thing once more. So listen:

"You are Wuntvor, apprentice to Ebenezum, sent here to try
and enlist Mother Duck in your cause. Unfortunately, Mother
Duck is a stubborn, willful woman, and will not even listen to
your pleas. Therefore, you were in the midst of escaping when
the old woman once again got you under her spell."

Wuntvor blinked. "You're right. I'm starting to remember.
How can I ever thank you?"

"Think nothing of it," the sword assured him. "It's totally
self-preservation. Once these fairy tales get going, you always
end up whipping out your sword—that's me—for one thing or
another. It always ends in blood." The sword shivered in the
lad's hand. "Or worse than blood."

"Worse than blood?" the lad asked, intrigued despite his
confusion.

"Ichor," the sword explained miserably. "Hair oil. Unicorn saliva."

Wuntvor nodded. He was beginning to recall some of those incidents as well. He closed his eyes, trying to will the last remnants of the spell away.

"Once upon—" He clamped his mouth shut. Those words had come to his lips unbidden.

"Mother Duck's controlling spell," the sword explained. "You must refrain from saying those words at all cost, or you will be under her power forever. But come. Let us try to free the others."

Wuntvor looked to the rest of those in the clearing, all wandering about, mumbling over and over those four fateful words.

"Indeed," the lad asked his weapon as they approached the others, "if this woman's sorcery is so powerful, how did you manage to escape?"

"By my very definition," the sword patiently explained. "I'm a magical device. Spells bounce right off my shiny blade."

"Indeed," the lad responded. Why did that explanation sound so familiar?

"Quickly, now," the sword cautioned, "we have to awaken the others and flee. I want to be done with this as soon as possible, before any—" The sword paused, as if it found it difficult to say the next word. "—bloodshed begins."

"Very well," Wuntvor agreed. But before he could take a dozen paces, he heard a strange, high-pitched laugh emanating from the edge of the nearby forest.

"Hee, hee, hee! Hello, my dearies," the strange voice continued. "I've come with a present for Wuntvor."

The others in the clearing all turned toward the voice.

"Doom?" said one particularly large fellow.

"Buckles and laces!" exclaimed one who was particularly short.

"Yes," the old lady continued as she stepped into their midst. "Hee, hee, hee! I've brought a special basket of apples for my special Eternal Apprentice."

"It's Mother Duck!" the sword whispered.

The old woman smiled as she caught Wuntvor's eye. The lad took a step away, not knowing what to expect.

"Now, now," the woman said reassuringly. "There's no reason to be afraid. I've just brought you all some food."

She pulled back her dark shawl to reveal a basket of apples she had hung on one of her arms. They were unlike any apples Wuntvor had ever seen. In fact, they glowed bright green in the darkness.

"Don't they look delicious?" Mother Duck asked encouragingly. "So plump, so crisp, so sweet. Hee, hee, hee! Wouldn't you like to be biting into one right now?"

Wuntvor swallowed and backed away again. He wasn't sure he wanted to eat any fruit that contained its own light source.

A wolf in a green cap ran up to the old woman. "Hey," the beast said, "if I can't eat anything else, at least one of these will stave off my hunger." He snatched a piece of fruit from the basket.

"How dare you!" Mother Duck began. Wuntvor flinched at her anger. Glancing apologetically at the lad, she spoke to the wolf in more soothing tones. "Oh, I suppose it's all right. You must be hungry. I've neglected to put any meals in any of today's fairy tales, haven't I? We just have to make sure that Wuntvor gets one." She waved the basket in the lad's direction. "Not that there's anything special about these apples. No, no, except that they are especially delicious! Hee, hee, hee!"

"Doom." The large fellow lumbered over to the basket and extracted an apple. "I am famished."

"Buckles and laces!" The very small fellow jumped into the basket, deftly pushing a piece of fruit over the rim. "Brownies need to maintain their strength!" He leapt after the falling apple.

Mother Duck stopped short. In the strange, green light of the apples, she looked very upset.

"If another of you touches my apples, I will smite—" She paused when she noticed that Wuntvor was rapidly backing away once again.

"Oh, dear," she said after a moment, her voice much kinder. "Hee, hee, hee! I'm afraid I'm unnecessarily cross. Mother Duck shouldn't stay up so late. It's after her bedtime!" She once again pushed the basket toward Wuntvor. "There's more than enough fruit to go around. But everyone should wait until

Wuntvor gets an apple of his own. It's only polite."

The wolf took a noisy bite from his apple.

"Ummmm!" he exclaimed. "That's delici—"

He fell on his face before he could finish the sentence and began to snore loudly.

"Speaking of inappropriate manners!" Mother Duck exclaimed, pointing disdainfully at the sleeping beast. "He eats before everyone is served, and then immediately takes a nap! The nerve of some creatures! He'll never get to be in any more of my fairy tales, let me tell you!"

She took another step toward Wuntvor. A fair damsel sneaked up behind her and lifted an apple from the basket.

"Hee, hee, hee! Now, my dear, sweet boy. I've brought these apples just for you. I know you've been stubborn, not wanting to say certain words. But Mother Duck isn't angry. Oh, no. Hee, hee, hee. And to show you how pleased I am with you, I just want you to take one tiny little bite out of one tiny little apple. Mother Duck will feel so much better if you do."

"In-indeed," Wuntvor managed, "I do not wish to."

The old woman stood there for a moment, staring without expression at the youngster. A shortish fellow hidden within a huge robe reached out and took a piece of fruit.

"You do not wish to?" she asked at last, the sweetness in her voice evaporating with every word. "You are in Mother Duck's kingdom, and you do not wish to?" She laughed again, but it had a darker sound than before. "You come here, unannounced, unasked for, because of some stupid quest far beneath my notice. And now you refuse to obey my wishes? Oh, I'll grant you that you've brought along some interesting fodder for my fairy tales, but that is not enough! There are orders that must be obeyed! There are apples that must be eaten!"

She thrust the basket forward. Wuntvor could smell the apples now; they were almost beneath his nose. They smelled very sweet, almost sickeningly so, as if their green skins were made of sugar. As sweet as they were, though, he wanted one. He couldn't remember the last time he had eaten. Then again, he couldn't remember a lot of things.

His mouth started to water.

"Why don't you take an apple?" the old woman demanded. "Just one small bite, a few seconds, and it will be over. I think I deserve at least that much, after all I've done for you." She tried to smile encouragement. It didn't work.

She sighed, a scowl once again dominating her face. "You force me to become personally involved in one of my own fairy stories, just so I might rescue my kingdom from the damage this sleeping wolf has done! I have never spent so much time fooling around with my stories—and you know I am a Fairy Tale Professional!" She paused, doing her best to control her temper. "I suppose you have done things for me as well. Heaven knows, you have opened new vistas, new possibilities in which I might ply my traditional tales. I am grateful for that much. Heaven knows I've never been able to call upon Death the way you seem able to. But I think it is time for those possibilities I keep seeing to become fairy tale reality—Now!"

She stared at the lad, and her eyes seemed to glow with a cold, green fire, much the same color as the shining apples.

"Think handsome prince," she whispered.

Wuntvor began to sweat.

"Um—," he managed. "Indeed?"

Mother Duck laughed sourly. "Still you resist me. Can't you see that it is hopeless? I am the supreme ruler of all I survey. Once you enter my kingdom, you are mine. For as long as I want you, you are mine, even if that is the rest of your life."

The green glow in her eyes intensified. Wuntvor couldn't look away. He found his lips and tongue moving of their own volition.

"Once upon—," the lad began. "Ow!"

Somehow, his sword had slapped him in the thigh. Wuntvor looked down at his weapon.

"Don't look at her!" the sword demanded. "I guarantee you, it'll lead to bloodshed!"

"That does it!" Mother Duck raged. "You seem to have some sort of incredible dumb luck that always saves you. Well, it won't save you this time! Eternal Apprentice or no, you are going to eat one of my apples!"

She swung the basket behind her, as if getting ready to fling the fruit in Wuntvor's face. So intent was she on her retribution, though, that she did not notice that the dragon had somehow maneuvered his great bulk directly behind her. The great reptile caught the swinging basket deftly between his formidable teeth, tipping the wicker just so, allowing the five remaining apples to slide down his gullet.

"What?" Mother Duck stared at her empty basket in disbelief. "Gone? Every one of my delicious, very special apples gone?" She glared at Wuntvor. "You will not escape my wrath this easily! Wait right there! I will be back as soon as I reload!"

There was a substantial crash as the dragon fell behind her. The huge reptile began to snore loudly. Mother Duck grumbled under her breath as she stormed off around the sleeping lizard.

"Well," the sword in Wuntvor's hand said, "I guess we showed her."

"Indeed," the lad answered, still not quite sure what he had done. "What do we do now?"

"Hmmm," the sword considered. "Well, now that Mother Duck's gone, I suppose I can resume the introductions. I, incidentally, am called Cuthbert. In case you forget again, my name is tastefully inscribed on the side of my blade. You had forgotten, hadn't you? We definitely have to get you out of this fairy tale business. Now, swing me around toward the others, and I'll reintroduce you, let us hope for the last time."

Wuntvor did as the sword bade, turning the blade toward his companions, who all seemed to have fallen to the ground.

"Oh, dear," the sword moaned. "Everyone seems to be asleep. How can we escape when everyone is asleep?"

Wuntvor frowned. Cuthbert was correct. The entire company was quietly snoring, surrounded by half-eaten apples.

"Oh, well," Cuthbert continued. "I suppose I'll identify them all anyway. It'll save time when they're done with their nap. Point me from left to right, will you? Yes, there's Hendrek the warrior and Snarks the demon, and Alea is the damsel's name. That large reptile in the middle is called Hubert. Oh, yes, and the wolf's name is Jeffrey, but you don't have to worry about him. I'm afraid he wouldn't make much of a companion. His appetite would get in the way.

"Oh, dear." Cuthbert hesitated before speaking again, his voice much less certain. "I'm afraid I don't recognize the gentleman standing over on the far right." The sword glowed faintly, as if it might illuminate the stranger. "If you might come a

little bit forward, sir? I'm afraid we swords don't see all that
well in the moonlight."

"Gladly," replied a voice that sounded like dead leaves blowing in the wind.

"Oh, dear," the sword remarked. "I believe I recognize him
now."

So did Wuntvor.

EIGHTEEN

A wizard always attracts a crowd. The minute magic starts, huge quantities of people are attracted, all asking questions and jostling for a better view. It is not considered good form, however, to use your magic to banish these masses and give yourself quieter working conditions. Rather you should accept your lot, and consider the publicity value of spells performed before a large and grateful public. And of course, performing magic becomes even more fulfilling when you have already charged a nominal admission fee.

—*The Teachings of Ebenezum*, VOLUME V

I came to my senses all at once. It was amazing the way Death could do that for me.

The spectre walked forward to meet us. The night had, of course, grown suddenly cold.

"At last," Death whispered, "I have you alone, in a situation where I think we shall not be interrupted."

What was Death talking about? "But I am not alone!" I waved to the cluster of sleeping companions that surrounded us. "We are in the middle of a crowd."

The spectre laughed, the sound of small songbirds drowning in a whirlpool.

"Yes, a crowd—a sleeping crowd," he told me gently. "You do not know very much of Death, do you? Well, of course you wouldn't—you are the Eternal Apprentice, who has cheated me at every turn. You are the Eternal Apprentice, who always manages to elude me despite my best efforts, instead constantly being reborn to another bumbling life! You are the Eternal Apprentice, whose very existence makes a mockery of all my works and all I stand for—" The spectre stopped himself. "Pardon. There is no reason to be upset. I have you at last. There is no escape. I will show you that Death is a gentleman, and answer your question."

He waved at the crowd with a skeletal hand. "Your companions sleep, a deep, drugged slumber. They cannot help you now, for as long as they sleep, they are half in my kingdom already, and I will assure their continued somnambulance." Death sighed, the sound of dead grass blown by the winter wind. "It is nice of us to meet at night, for this is the time Death feels most comfortable walking through the world. It is fitting that I should take you now, at my leisure, after I have stalked you for so long."

"Indeed," I commented, trying to determine some way to stay alive, if only for a few more minutes. I sidled over to the deeply snoring Hendrek and kicked him gently in the breastplate. Hendrek didn't react. I kicked him harder.

"Ow!" I had managed to hurt my big toe in the process. Hendrek still did not respond, not even a muffled "Doom." He snored on, oblivious to my predicament.

Death laughed drily, the sound of beetles eating at a rotting carcass. "You see now that I have won."

"I am not yours yet!" I yelled, backing away from the spectre.

"That's telling him!" Cuthbert shouted encouragingly. "Now what say we get out of here?"

"Must we be tiresome?" a voice said behind me. I whirled around to see Death barely an arm's length away. "I have told you before that escape is impossible. Death is everywhere. I am inevitable."

The spectre spread his arms wide, pointing to a pair of trees on either side. A wind came from somewhere, perhaps even from inside the spectre's bonelike fingers. Leaves whipped about in the gale, curling inward like small animals in pain. The wind seemed to leech the color from them as well, turning green to yellow to driest brown, the leaves at last ripping away from their branches to be carried away by the death wind until all the tree limbs were bare. But the trees were changing as well. Where once they were young and vibrant, only a few years beyond saplings, now they became twisted and gnarled, filled with a crawling rot that seemed to spread from the inside out, causing limbs to fall and bark to decompose before my eyes until, where once two strong trees had stood, now there was nothing but stumps and dust.

Death's laughter boomed through the forest, the sound of a thunderstorm that would destroy everything in its path.

"Maybe it's time for me to go back in my scabbard," Cuthbert suggested.

"Yes," the spectre chortled. "You can run. You can hide. It will do you no good. It won't do anybody any good. As of now, Death will take anybody he wants, at any time he wants. And that includes the Eternal Apprentice!"

He reached for Wuntvor. "Come. Take my hand. You entered this world alone, but you will leave it with me. As long as I have savored this moment, still I promise you, it will be over in an instant."

"Oh, no, it won't!" a wondrously mellifluous voice interrupted.

"Who is that?" Death raved. "Who disturbs my ultimate moment?"

"I do!" And the unicorn cantered forward. In the darkness, the wondrous beast's coat looked as if it were made of moonlight. It waved its shimmering horn in my direction. "You cannot take him. The lad and I have—" The unicorn paused significantly. "—unfinished business."

"I should have known." Death's voice rose like the howling gale that brings a hurricane. "I come here to find all his companions unconscious, leaving the Eternal Apprentice alone, without aid. I should have taken him in that instant, but no, I was too confident, too willing to gloat over my victory. I am Death, after all, used to having my way with all normal, mortal creatures. But I forget that the creature I want now may not be mortal, and certainly isn't normal!"

"Indeed," I replied, seeking a way to further demoralize the spectre. "Come here, O noble unicorn. To my side!"

"To his side?" the unicorn whispered, its soulful brown eyes filling with tears. "He wants me by his side. You don't know how long I've waited to hear those words."

Slowly, carefully—as if the beast feared that, should it move too quickly, it might wake from its newfound dream—the unicorn trotted to my side.

The spectre made a noise halfway between a moan and a snicker. Death seemed to be trembling.

"Do not think for an instant—," he said at last, each word hissing forth as if spoken by a snake about to strike, "do not think I am not prepared for this eventuality. So it is the middle of the night, when most intelligent creatures do not venture forth. So it is a very special night, when most of your companions rest here in a drugged sleep, unable to help their beloved Eternal Apprentice. Still, I knew my conquest might not be easy, that somehow, some way, you would find a method to try to thwart your destiny."

The spectre's bony hand pointed shakily at the unicorn. "Notice that I said you might *try* to thwart your destiny! For, as surely as I have claimed a million billion souls, I swear this night that I shall add the Eternal Apprentice to my collection, no matter what the obstacles!"

"Eep eep!" came a cry in the night.

"What was that?" Death shrieked, pulling his robes close about his skeletal form.

"Indeed?" I said, surprised by the spectre's reaction. "It is only one of my ferrets."

"Only one?" Death whispered. "Then why have I heard that cry, over and over, ever since that small brown creature attacked me when we met earlier today?"

"Indeed?" I thought fast. That would have been at least a couple of attempts on my life ago, when I had thought fondly of my ferret, and it had appeared.

"Eep eep eep!" the ferret called.

"What is this creature?" Death demanded. "You must tell me!"

I shrugged. "He is naught but a magic ferret."

"Magic?" Death stared wildly out into the night. "How could a ferret be magic?"

"I conjured him, using a magic hat—," I began.

"A ferret, created by the Eternal Apprentice?" Death shook so violently I could hear his bones rattle. "I should have known! Only a ferret created by an immortal could follow Death into his kingdom! Well, this will happen no more! I will end this haunting once and for all. I will take you, and the unicorn, and the enchanted ferret as well. Death will win this night!" The spectre chuckled, his confidence returning. "But then, Death always wins."

I felt the unicorn's soft pelt against my leg.

"If we have to go," the beast moaned magnificently, "at least we go together. I wouldn't want it any other way."

"Indeed?" I remarked, because I was beginning to formulate a plan. "Ferret, to my side!"

"Eep eep eep!" the little creature cried as it streaked across the clearing. I saw Death flinch as it passed.

"Yes," I said to the small animal as it nuzzled my shoe. "We might as well all be together, as Death has suggested."

Death grinned, pleased at my acquiescence. He stepped forward to take all three of us.

"After all," I continued, "being together like this makes it so much easier to call the others."

Death stopped. "The others?"

I nodded. "This is not my only ferret."

Death took a step back. "It isn't?"

"No," I answered. "It is only one of hundreds."

"Hundreds?" Death whispered. "You have hundreds of magic ferrets? Look into my eyes, Apprentice. It is impossible to lie to Death!"

I did my best to gaze into the spectre's deep eye sockets. For I was not lying. I did have a virtually limitless supply of ferrets. Of course, all but one of them were still back in Vushta, with no way to join us here. But I did not intend to tell Death that particular fact.

"You do have hundreds!" Death moaned. "Hundreds of ferrets, overrunning my peaceful kingdom?"

My plan was working. Death's sudden panic at my magic ferrets entering his kingdom had unnerved him enough so I was sure that he would think twice about taking our lives.

"But, no," Death said, shaking himself. "I am overreacting. There is only one ferret here. If I take you quickly, perhaps you would not have time to call the rest of them. And even if you could, perhaps it would be worth it to have hundreds of eeping ferrets in my kingdom, if I also had the Eternal Apprentice!" He reached out both his arms to take us all. "For, no matter what happens, I have sworn to take you tonight."

"Indeed?" I said, more than a bit upset at this turn of events. It had not taken him long to think twice. Unfortunately, my plan went no further.

"And what exactly is going on here?" a commanding female voice called from behind me.

Death looked past my shoulder. "I knew it would happen like this! I've had any number of chances to take the Eternal Apprentice. But do I? No, I end up talking with him, instead. Discussing ferrets! And then, who shows up, but yet another companion that I must take to my dark domain."

"Another companion?" the female voice asked.

"Do not deny it!" Death shrieked. "The Eternal Apprentice draws companions the way rotting meat draws flies!"

"It's bad enough that Death is going to get us all," Cuthbert wailed. "Do we have to listen to his metaphors as well?"

"How dare you call me a companion!" the voice demanded. "I am Mother Duck! I was simply bringing Wuntvor his apples."

"No matter who you claim to be," Death replied, "I must take you. For to take the Eternal Apprentice, I am risking chaos. I can leave no living witnesses."

"You will do no such thing!" Mother Duck exclaimed, walking forward so that she stood between me and Death. "This is my kingdom, and whoever enters it acts only on my command!"

Death laughed again. I did not like the way he was regaining confidence. "You, then, are the legendary mistress of fairy tales who rules the Eastern Kingdoms? You will be a welcome addition to my domain. Concocting fairy stories seems very much like a game. Have I told you that I am very fond of games?"

"You seem awfully sure of yourself for an interloper," the old woman complained, "but we'll soon take care of that. Look into my eyes."

"Ah. That sounds like a fine game." Death smiled and did as she wished.

Nothing happened. Mother Duck turned away in frustration.

"How can I bend you to my will when you don't have any eyes to stare into?"

"Death is beyond the petty concerns of mortals," the spectre replied casually. "But come now. I have dawdled enough with all of you. You must join with me, before there are any further distractions."

"See?" a voice came from the forest. "They are so having a party, and they didn't invite us!"

"Really, Touchy," another voice chided, "we should be above that sort of thing."

"Oh, wow," a third voice added as the Seven Other Dwarves strode into the clearing.

"I don't believe this," Death whispered, the sound of ice freezing forever.

"Oh, look," Smarmy said, reading from a piece of parchment. "It is our good friend, the handsome prince. But look again! He has fallen asleep."

Smarmy looked up at me and frowned. "Oh, my. Excuse me if I'm wrong, but aren't you supposed to be the handsome prince?"

"He's the handsome prince?" Nasty asked sarcastically. "Pardon me, but is there a new definition of the word *handsome?*"

Smarmy looked about at the bodies littering the clearing. "But it appears that everybody else has fallen asleep instead!"

"Oh, it just figures that *our* fairy tale would go wrong—" Touchy hesitated. "Why, Mother Duck!"

"Mother Duck?" Smarmy dropped the piece of paper to wring his hands. "Why, so it is. I'm sure Touchy didn't mean anything by his fairy tale remark, Mother Duck."

"Certainly not, Mother Duck," Touchy hastily added.

"Always a pleasure working for you, Mother Duck," Nasty chimed in.

"Oh, wow, Mother Duck," Spacey remarked.

"And may I humbly say what a great pleasure it is to see

you, Mother Duck?" Smarmy continued. "As you can see, we were following your instructions to the letter."

"Yes, you were, my most excellent dwarves," the old woman replied with a smile that evaporated when she turned to look at me, "unlike certain others I can name!"

"This must end," Death intoned with a force that stopped all other conversation. He then turned to look at me as well. "You are almost beyond belief. I'm sure I could meet you in the most desolate place on earth, and it would immediately become as crowded as Vushta on market day! Well, the walls of chaos may rip asunder, and I will be so tired that no one will die for a week, but I will take you all."

He walked toward me, holding out both his hands. "I have long ago stopped doubting that you were the Eternal Apprentice. Now, I only wonder at what a grand addition you will be to my kingdom. But come, we have dawdled long enough—"

He paused. The clearing was filled with the beating of a drum.

> "Guxx Unfufadoo, curious demon,
> Wants to know what's going on here,
> Wants to speak to his friend Wuntvor,
> Wants to go on back to Vushta!"

"No!" Death screamed in frustration. "No, no, no! This gets worse with every passing second!" The spectre shuddered. "But I will *still* take all of you. The paperwork will be staggering, but while the declaimer is an imposing fellow, the one beating the drum is small enough. I think I can still fit both of them in. Come now! I will not wait another—"

There were twin explosions in our midst.

"Indeed," remarked the shoe that had just appeared.

"It's really time for Brownie Power!" His Brownieship added.

"It's the talking shoe again?" Death seemed overwhelmed. "What can you do with a talking shoe?"

"A lot of things!" Mother Duck replied, obviously intrigued. "For one thing there's this old lady I know who keeps having these kids and doesn't know what to do with them—"

"I was speaking rhetorically," Death informed her drily. "I

know what I will do with this shoe, and the little person who has arrived as well. I will take them to my kingdom. I will take you all to my kingdom, though it shall tax my powers to the utmost." He looked to the heavens. "Come storm! Come wind and thunder and rain! Give me your energy, for I have many to kill!"

The howling was faint at first, as if it came from a great distance. But it grew quickly, doubling in intensity with every heartbeat, until it sounded like the anguish of a million souls. Black clouds rushed overhead, blotting out the moon and stars, making the dark night darker still. There was a rumbling in the distance.

Death laughed.

"I have you now!" he roared. "Although it will take all my resources, I will gain the strength to transport every one of you to my kingdom in an instant."

The clouds crashed together overhead. The distant rumbling was coming closer, gaining definition so that it sounded like someone beating the world's largest drum.

"Odd." Death paused, as if even he were startled by the noise. "But it does not matter. Perhaps it is some manifestation of my power that even I am not yet aware of." He returned his gaze to the sky.

"Come lightning!"

The clouds above crashed together with resounding force, sending out bright white flashes where they met. Death's laughter doubled.

The booming sound was coming closer, too.

There came a crash overhead so great that I fell to my knees and covered my ears. A bolt of lightning streaked from the clouds, straight for Death.

I could feel the booming sound. It shook the ground where I knelt.

Death's laughter became as loud as the thunder as he was bathed in the white fire. Then the lightning was gone, but Death glowed from within, his bonelike face so bright that you could not look at it for more than a second.

"Now," Death whispered in a voice far louder than a shout. "The time is—"

The booming sound intensified, now as loud as Death, shaking the whole clearing with every thundering beat.

The booming stopped.

Death looked up. A single word came from on high.

"Oops!"

And Death screamed.

NINETEEN

Any working magician will encounter situations which are potentially embarrassing, such as being trapped at a party with your spouse's relatives, or potentially deadly, such as finding yourself in front of a murderous crowd when a very important spell has backfired, or even both, such as being trapped with a crowd of your spouse's murderous relatives. It therefore behooves the mage to always have a couple of escape spells handy so that he might quickly exit these situations. But the truly professional wizard will go one better, devising another spell (and this is especially important with spouse's relatives) that proves he did not go into those situations at all.

—*The Teachings of Ebenezum*, VOLUME XXII

Death was gone. And dawn was breaking over the Eastern Kingdoms.

Mother Duck groaned. "That was quite a night. With you around, I doubt I shall ever get any sleep. But there are newcomers to my kingdom I must greet. Now what have I done with my apples?"

"Breakfast," Richard remarked, turning the basket over so that all the green, glowing apples fell upon his tongue. He swallowed them with a single gulp.

Mother Duck groaned again, flinging her hands up toward the heavens. "What else can happen to me now? Oh, Richard!" She sat down heavily upon a tree stump. "I would be more upset with you if I was not so exhausted."

"Oops!" Richard replied. "Have I done something wrong?" And then he burped.

But Mother Duck waved him to silence as she stood again and walked over to my master, still hidden within his shoe.

"Welcome to my kingdom, oh talking shoe," she greeted Ebenezum. "I will have to find a use for you."

"Indeed?" my master replied. "Well, I shall have to return once you have made up your mind."

And with that, both my master and His Brownieship disappeared.

"Richard!" Mother Duck screamed, suddenly furious.

"Yes, Mother Duck?" the giant said with a yawn.

"That talking shoe is trying to escape me!" she replied. "No one escapes Mother Duck!"

"Yes, Mother Duck," a chorus of voices added all around me.

"Track down that shoe, Richard," Mother Duck commanded, "and bring it to me!"

Richard yawned again. "Couldn't I take a nap first?"

"No sleeping on the job!" the old woman snapped. "Bring me that shoe *now!*"

"Yes, Mother Duck." Barely able to keep his eyes open, the giant staggered off into the woods.

"Now I will have to see what I can do with the rest of you." She looked at me first. "Since you seem destined never to eat one of my special apples, we will have to revise the plot slightly."

The wolf moaned in his sleep. The dragon shifted, his tail propelling the heavily robed Snarks a dozen paces. Alea sat up and rubbed her eyes.

Mother Duck nodded sagely. "The effects of my special sauce seem to be wearing off. We'd better get to work!"

"Happily ever after," I whispered. I had been able to avoid

Mother Duck's control for hours now. Still, I wondered if I could survive a direct confrontation. I concentrated hard on anything I could think of besides those four words: Norei, my master, the crisis in Vushta, the threat of the Netherhells. Once—no, I didn't want to think of that word! My mind had to dwell on other, more intricate things: Snarks's worst insults, Guxx's most elaborate poetry, Damsel and Dragon's production numbers.

That seemed to work, at least for a moment.

Mother Duck frowned. "Wasn't there a unicorn around here a minute ago?" She covered her mouth as she yawned. So she was tired, too. It seemed to be affecting her concentration. I felt the pressure lift from my skull.

All the sleepers were stirring now. Alea had gotten to her feet, while the wolf sat up and stretched and Hubert tentatively flapped his wings. Snarks rolled around on the ground, some-how lost deep within his voluminous robes, while the Brownie seemed to have embarked on some sort of a morning exercise program, leaping from place to place with a great deal of shouting and arm waving.

I sat down on the hard-packed earth. I realized it had been a long time since I had slept. All this stretching and yawning was making me feel even more exhausted. My eyes were heavy, but I wouldn't let them close. I was still afraid of Mother Duck's powers, and what might happen if I let my concentration slip, even for an instant.

"Look!" Mother Duck called triumphantly. "The handsome prince is getting drowsy! Perhaps we can get this fairy tale moving after all!"

Handsome prince? What handsome prince? I tried blinking, but for some reason my eyes, while willing enough to close, did not wish to open again.

"We'll have to start right now!" the old woman exclaimed. "There's no time for me to cast any spells." She barely repressed another yawn. "Also, I do not know if I have the energy. I don't want things going wrong once more. You'll just all have to be on your best behavior."

I breathed deeply. There was something about this handsome prince thing that seemed familiar. Wait a minute. Didn't that have something to do with me?

"First, you see, " Mother Duck instructed, "is the kiss to wake him."

Oh. I breathed more easily, and stopped struggling to open my eyes. Kiss to wake me? That didn't sound so bad.

"And then, of course," Mother Duck continued, "the prince will begin his terrible trials of violence to rescue his kingdom from the evil curse."

"Terrible trials of violence?" a voice squeaked nearby. Something whipped sharply against my side. "Hurry up! It's time to wake up! It's time to get out of here!"

"Ow!" I exclaimed, my eyes opening so suddenly that I had difficulty focusing on my surroundings. I managed to blink more normally. The bruise on my thigh had brought me back to wakefulness.

"Well, are we getting out of here or not?"

I looked in the direction of the voice and saw that I still held my sword in my limp fingers.

"Oh, drat!" Mother Duck yelled. "He's waking up. Well, we'd best start the fairy tale *now!* Let's see—um— Once upon a time there was a handsome young prince, who had been put to sleep by a poisoned apple given to him by an evil witch. Now this witch wanted to rule the prince's fair kingdom, and so brought forth three terrible trials upon the land. The people despaired—um—that is, all except—um—one fair damsel, who knew if she could wake the prince, all could still be saved." The old woman clapped her hands. "There. Not bad for off the top of my head. Always get the action going quickly—that's what I always say. So where's the beautiful damsel?"

Alea pointed to herself. "Do you mean me?"

Mother Duck tapped her foot impatiently. "No, I mean all the other beautiful damsels who are sitting around this clearing. Hurry up and kiss the prince!"

"Wuntie?" Alea asked tentatively.

"Do I have to cast a spell?" Mother Duck inquired darkly.

"Oh, no!" Alea replied, dimpling prettily. "I like kissing Wuntie!"

She skipped happily in my direction.

"Wuntie!" she called, getting into her role. "I am coming to kiss you awake!"

"Pardon me," I apologized to my sword as I sheathed it. I often was not at my best around Alea, and I thought it prudent to avoid any accident. Still, I supposed I would have to let her kiss me, even though my heart still belonged to Norei, my own true love. After all, I reasoned, a kiss like this was a small thing, and there was no reason to needlessly anger Mother Duck before I could find some opportunity for me and my company to escape.

I therefore stood my ground and puckered, fully ready to take the consequences.

"Kiss him now!" Mother Duck commanded. "Remember, this is the beginning of the story, so make it a good one!"

Alea ran forward, flinging her arms wide.

I am not precisely sure what happened next. Perhaps it was that I was still not fully awake. Whatever the cause, I managed to misjudge Alea's approach. Somehow, my right arm got in the way of her face.

"Ooh!" the damsel exclaimed. "Watch the fingers, Wuntie!"

I pulled both arms back, trying to stammer an apology. It was then that I lost my balance.

"Kiss him!" Mother Duck demanded. "The story can't start unless you kiss him!"

But Alea's arms, seeking to hug me, instead embraced the empty air. I had fallen rather ungracefully to the ground, knocking the breath from my lungs.

"Exhaustion or no exhaustion, Mother Duck is becoming annoyed," the old woman announced. "Kiss him now, or I cast a spell."

I realized that, no matter what happened, our chances were far better as long as our lives were still under our own control. Therefore, winded though I was, I struggled quickly to my feet. Unfortunately, Alea seemed in as much of a hurry as myself and was rapidly bending down toward me, her lips puckered and at the ready.

Her jaw hit my forehead with a sharp crack. Both of us recoiled at the sudden pain. Just before the blow, however, I had felt Alea's lips brush across my forehead.

"Kiss him!" the old woman demanded. "Or you will feel the wrath of Mother Duck!"

"I did!" Alea protested, massaging her chin. I helpfully

pointed to where her lips had brushed my scalp.

Mother Duck shook her head disapprovingly. "That's no way to start a fairy story. We want a real kiss. We want passion. You're an actress. Act!"

Alea stopped stroking her jaw and managed a smile that still contained a bit of a wince.

"Oh, Wuntie," she emoted. "I have waited for this moment for so long."

"That's better," Mother Duck encouraged.

"Oh, Alea," I replied, for I felt something was expected of me. "Um— How pleasant it is to see you."

"Not so good," the old woman murmured. "But we'll let it pass. It's time for the hug."

Alea grabbed me. Her face was very close to mine, her curly blond hair brushing against my nose. It was getting very hot around here again.

"That's fine," Mother Duck commented. "So kiss him, and kiss him good. Now, let's see some tongues!"

"What is going on here?" another woman's voice cut through the morning air.

My heart leapt, as if it wished to escape from my ribcage and run to my beloved. For I recognized that voice.

It was Norei.

I pushed away from Alea with such suddenness that both of us fell in opposite directions.

"Who is this?" Mother Duck asked, her surprise temporarily conquering her annoyance.

My beloved surveyed all those in the clearing, her arms folded before her. Her gaze paused on the fallen Alea. "There is only so much a maiden can stand."

"If you say so," the old woman replied. "May I ask who you are?"

"I am Norei," my beloved replied, "daughter of one of the most powerful witch families in the Western Woods."

"A witch family? This gets more and more interesting with every passing minute," Mother Duck remarked. "Perhaps I will dispense with my control spells altogether. Who knows who, or what, will show up next?"

"Indeed!" I called, jumping up from the ground and drawing

my sword in one more or less fluid movement. Ignoring Cuthbert's startled cry, I rushed quickly to my beloved's side. I had been a prisoner in Mother Duck's kingdom long enough to know the true duplicitousness of her nature. I would protect Norei from the old woman's spells any way I could, though it might cost me my very life.

"Wuntvor?" Norei stared at me in delightful surprise, startled I am sure with the speed with which I reached her side. Her green eyes were opened wide, her beautiful lips slightly parted. I could not help myself.

I kissed her.

"At last!" Mother Duck exclaimed. "Let the fairy tale begin!"

TWENTY

When you are with your beloved, nothing can go wrong. Well, actually, some things can go wrong, I'm afraid I know that from experience—really, I guess, now that I think of it, all sorts of things can go wrong—Norei! Where are you going?

—*Some Thoughts on Apprenticeship,* by Wuntvor,
apprentice to Ebenezum,
greatest wizard in the Western Kingdoms
(a discarded early draft)

Norei and I clutched each other as the world around us was suddenly filled with smoke. Somewhere, far away, I heard Mother Duck's laughter.

"Oh, Wuntvor," my beloved whispered in my ear. "I know I shouldn't have shown myself. At least not yet. It's simply that you have been put through such indignities by that Mother Duck person. It was almost impossible to stand by when your life was repeatedly in danger. And then, when that Alea—" She paused, unable to continue.

"Do not worry, Norei," I replied with a conviction that I did

169

not truly feel. "Now that we are together, we have to win."

"Well, I hope so," she replied, not wholly convinced herself.
"Heaven knows why I get into these things with you, Wuntvor.
You can be the most exasperating man in the world."

I looked as deeply into Norei's eyes as the dissipating smoke
would allow. I knew, when she talked to me that way, that
she truly loved me. Sometime, when we were not in the middle
of an ongoing crisis, I would have to prove to her how much
that love meant to me.

"Doom." The word echoed all around as a large shape loomed
before us in the clearing. A summer breeze sprang up, whisking
the remaining smoke away in an instant.

Norei whistled. "This Mother Duck likes her special effects,
doesn't she?"

"Doom." The large warrior Hendrek appeared before us, the
cursed warclub Headbasher at his side. "I am the first trial."

"Hendrek?" I asked my large friend. "What trial?"

But the large warrior continued to advance on us, his only
reply another muttered "Doom." I tried to catch his eye, but
his face was without expression. I understood at once. Apparently, Mother Duck was still exerting her control on some of us.

I lifted my sword before me. "Hendrek, think what you are
doing. Don't force me to use this."

"Just what are you suggesting?" Cuthbert demanded. "Oh,
no matter how many times you have reassured me, I knew this
would happen! There's going to be blood!"

"Your sword is no match for this." Hendrek smiled unnatur-
ally, lifting his club.

"He's right, you know," Cuthbert interjected hurriedly.
"Other methods are called for. Methods that don't involve
swords."

"Come," the warrior beckoned, "and let me add you to my
list of victims."

"Oh, no you don't!" my beloved interjected. "If you attack
Wuntvor, you must attack me as well!"

What was Norei saying? I thrust my sword even farther
forward, ignoring the blade's whining pleas. I had to protect
my beloved!

"Doom," the warrior replied with a frown. "If that's the way
you want it." Taking a final step in our direction, he lifted

Headbasher high over his head.

Norei spoke a quick string of arcane syllables, snapping her fingers twice.

The warclub reversed direction and hit Hendrek's helmet with a resounding clang.

"Do—urk!" the warrior remarked as he crumpled to the ground.

"Simple violence-reversal spell," the young witch explained.

"I don't know if it should be going this way," an older woman's voice complained somewhere out in the forest.

"Now you know how I felt!" a gruff and wolfish voice replied.

"Mother Duck will not be defeated. It is time for the next trial! And—," she added, raising her voice, "if anyone uses magic to save the handsome prince, it will be their last act!"

"Norei!" I cried, frightened for my beloved.

But the young witch only smiled at my concern. "Do not worry, Wuntvor. As you said, we are together. We will think of something."

Once again, from out of nowhere, smoke surrounded us. It cleared even more quickly this time, to show us two demons, one of whom was already beating a drum.

The other demon seemed to hesitate. After a moment he started, as if he had been asleep on his feet, and cleared his throat, a truly horrendous sound. He spoke:

"Guxx—uh—Unfufadoo—er—hypnotized demon,
Um— Sees a prince who's ripe for beating,
Sees a prince who's—uh—ready to topple,
Sees someone who—um—will make an okay meal!"

Norei frowned. "Guxx!" she demanded. "The rhythm on that is terrible! Do you expect us to quake in fear with verse like that?"

"Um," Guxx replied, for he, too, seemed to be suffering from one of Mother Duck's spells. "I suppose not. Um—" He frowned, his oversized fangs making small marks in his lower lip and chin. "What do you suggest?"

"More active verbs," Norei suggested. "I mean, what do you do with your meals?"

"Oh, I see." The demon's hideous green tongue stuck out

of the corner of his mouth as he was temporarily lost in thought. He mumbled: "Guxx Unfufadoo, dada demon, / Sees a prince dadada beating, / Sees dadada dada topple—"

Guxx paused and smiled. "Yes, that's much better." He raised his voice and enunciated every word: "Sees a prince who's good for eat—"

Guxx Unfufadoo began to sneeze.

"A natural rhyming talent!" the drum-beating Brax proclaimed as the larger demon fell to the ground, the sneezing fit getting the better of him.

"There we go," Norei announced. "You've conquered your second trial. And without a bit of magic!"

"This is all wrong!" Mother Duck wailed from her hiding place. "Where have I failed?"

"You didn't put any talking wolves—," Jeffrey began.

"I know what it is," the old woman interrupted summarily. "I've been warned about it. It's Fairy Tale Fatigue. We storytellers always have to be aware of the syndrome." She heaved an exhausted sigh. "I had always thought myself beyond it—until now—until I met—these people."

"Think how much easier it would have been though," Jeffrey interjected, "if you had had the buffer of a talk—"

"One more word out of you—," Mother Duck screamed, "—and you're pumpernickel!" She called out to the rest of us: "I remind you, this is the handsome prince's story. Anyone who interferes with the third trial in any way will have to answer to me!"

And with that, we were once again surrounded by smoke.

"Norei!" I called to my beloved. "Behind me. I must face this trial alone."

"Wuntvor—," she began, but the protest died in her throat. She knew I was right. Our chances of escape, even victory, were far greater so long as we did not incur the wrath of Mother Duck.

I heard a great rumbling through the impenetrable fog before me. I knew, even before the smoke cleared, that it was the dragon.

"I have a question," Cuthbert's voice quailed from where I still held it before me. "If you're going to face this menace alone, isn't it time you sheathed your sword?"

"Perhaps you are right," I replied, for I had thought of a plan.

"I'm right? I'm actually right? There's not going to be bloo—" The sword's cries of jubilation were lost once he was back in the scabbard.

I looked up to see that the smoke had cleared. There, before me, the size of a castle or a medium large hill, was the fire-breathing reptile—the dragon that I was sure was under Mother Duck's spell.

Thick smoke curled from the dragon's nostrils as the lizard's tongue darted forward, searching, I was sure, for my oh-so-edible scent. The dragon breathed in, preparing to fry me where I stood.

It was now or never.

"Hey!" I cried aloft. "It's showtime!"

The dragon paused. I had to think fast.

I started to sing:

> "What do you say to a dragon,
>   When he's stomping you into the ground?
>   I know my answer for certain,
>   Dragon, I'll see you around!"

Hubert exhaled, but it was smoke, not fire. He shook his head, as if trying to throw off the rigors of Mother Duck's magic. I decided to try another verse.

> "What do you say to that reptile,
>   When confronted by old dragon fire?
>   You tell the lizard you're sorry,
>   But you just have to retire!"

Hubert's tail started to swing in time to my singing. I had him now! I quickly continued.

> "What do you say to a dragon,
>   When he waits for battle so hard?
>   Well, it seems that you just have to travel,
>   But maybe you'll send him a card!"

*   *   *

Hubert's whole body was swaying by now. It was time to finish it.

"Take it, dragon!" I screamed.

And Hubert began to dance, bounding happily back and forth across the clearing as I sang the verses once again. As I had hoped, theater was too strong in his blood. With luck, I had found something Mother Duck could never conquer.

"No, no, no—," the old woman began, bounding out from her hiding place behind the trees. She stopped to consider. "Well, I suppose it will have to do, at least for this run-through. Now, though, we have to find a suitable conclusion."

"Oops!" came a voice from high overhead.

"Richard!" Mother Duck looked up, infuriated. "Your timing is terrible. Can't you see we're busy?"

But the giant would not be deterred. "See what I've found!" Richard had the shoe.

"Really?" the old woman's anger vanished. "What a good giant. Quickly, Richard, tell me what's inside."

"Oops," the giant replied as he stuck his index finger in the shoe. He shifted the footwear around to peer inside.

"Uh," he answered at last, "leather, mostly."

"I know about the leather!" Mother Duck replied, exasperation once again entering her voice. "But there's something else in there, too. What is it?"

"Oh." Richard turned the shoe upside down and shook it. He looked inside one more time, then frowned miserably down at Mother Duck.

"Nothing," was his answer.

Nothing? What had happened to my master?

"Nothing?" the old woman demanded. "That isn't possible!"

And then the earth began to quake.

"It cannot be!" Mother Duck raged.

But it was. I recognized all the signs: the violent tremors, the great clouds of dust, the sudden appearance of crevices in the earth.

And then the shaking stopped, and the dust cleared. There was the table with the five demons.

"Vushta!" the gavel demon cried in triumph. "We have you at last!"

But the demons' cheers died when they saw the old woman.

"Uh-oh," the gavel demon remarked.

"That's it," Mother Duck replied, all too casually. "You will never see the Netherhells again."

The demons all started talking at once.

"But Mother Duck, there was wizard magic—"

"Lots of it, Mother Duck—"

"And witch magic, too, Mother Duck—"

"Richard?" the old woman called to the giant. "I need your assistance."

"Oops!" The giant dropped the shoe and lumbered toward the committee.

"I see your master's plan!" Norei clapped me on the shoulder. "Oh, how brilliant!" She grabbed my hand and pulled me toward the fallen shoe. "Quickly, Wuntvor, we must get inside!"

I knew there was no time for questions. I did as my beloved bade.

At the far end of the clearing, Mother Duck and Richard faced the committee.

"Please, Mother Duck—," the demons pleaded.

"There's no other magic going on *anywhere,* Mother Duck—"

"We'll make a deal with you, Mother Duck! You show us where Vushta is, and we'll split it with you, fifty-fifty." The demon tried to smile ingratiatingly. Richard lumbered another step. "Uh, sixty-forty?"

But the old woman was unmoved by their pleas. "I do not want Vushta. I want my kingdom demon-free!"

We reached the shoe. Norei turned to the others in the clearing. "All of you," she called, "flee now, while Mother Duck is occupied. It is part of the wizard's plan!"

All those in the clearing fled. Norei scaled quickly up the shoe, using the eyelets for handholds and footholds. I followed as soon as she had dropped inside. I took a final look at the combatants before I, too, entered the footwear.

"Don't force us to get rough, Mother Duck—," one of the demons wailed.

"You'd better watch out, Mother Duck—," another added.

"We can boil blood, Mother Duck—," the demon in the flowered hat insisted.

The old woman sneered at their threats. "I don't think there's going to be any boiling around here. I think it's time to bake, instead. Richard?"

Norei pulled at my pants leg. I dropped down inside the shoe. The interior, while large enough to fit my master, seemed a little snug for two. I felt myself being pressed close to Norei.

"Quickly, Wuntvor!" my beloved insisted, gently pushing me away. "The words!"

Oh, that was right. The words! Now what were they? It was hard to breathe in these close confines. I managed to inhale anyway, and spoke:

"Happily ever after."

Nothing happened.

I saw Norei frowning in the dim light, her lips beautiful even in concentration.

"Why didn't they work?" she wondered. "They must have been muffled by the shoe leather. Poke your head out and try again. And say them slowly and distinctly."

I did as my beloved bade, climbing up so that my mouth was just above the top of the shoe. I was more exposed this way, though. I knew I would have to speak quickly, before Mother Duck could act.

"Happily—," I began.

"What's that?" Mother Duck asked, turning her head.

". . . ever—," I continued.

"Oh, no!" the old woman screamed. "The fairy tale! I didn't stop—"

". . . after!" I concluded. There was another puff of smoke. I was thrown back inside the shoe. Norei grabbed my hand as the giant footwear lurched off the ground.

We seemed to be flying.

TWENTY-ONE

"At least that's over."

—Final remarks made by Ebenezum,
greatest mage in the Western Kingdoms,
upon at last discovering an exit from
the secret passageways that actually led
outside the castle of King Snerdlot the
Vengeful. Rumor has it that, despite the
rigors of the night, the wizard managed
to stagger clear of the castle and its
surroundings, tactfully ignoring the
dozens of love notes thrown by Queen
Vivazia and her handmaidens until he
had reached the safety of the forest.

When we came out of the shoe, there was a rainbow overhead.

His Brownieship beamed up at us. "Is that Brownie Power or what?"

Norei had explained my master's plan as we had flown. At the first likely diversion during Mother Duck's tale, he and His Brownieship would find a means to transport me beyond the ruler of the Eastern Kingdom's power. The shoe was an ideal vehicle for that transportation, and when Ebenezum stayed around within it long enough to engage Mother Duck's curiosity, he guaranteed that it would be brought, without even having to use magic, back to Wuntvor by Mother Duck's minions. Then, once I was inside, all I had to do was shout three words to end the fairy tale, and His Brownieship did the rest.

I smiled down at the small fellow in the leather crown.

"Indeed," I replied, trying to place our exact location. We were still in the Eastern Woods, but in one of the clearings we had visited earlier, where we had first destroyed one of the dwarves' warning signs. I could still hear the sounds of distant battle, and I discovered that, if I craned my neck, I could see the top of the giant's head.

"We should move quickly," I announced. "We need to get out of here before the battle ends."

"Oh, it'll take them awhile," Smarmy announced as he and the other dwarves entered the clearing.

"It always does!" Snooty added.

"Indeed?" I replied. "This has happened before?"

"Regularly!" the dwarves answered in unison.

"This could take weeks!" Nasty shouted.

"And what do we get to do?" Touchy chimed in. "Sit on our hands!"

"Wuntvor?" my beloved interjected. "I still think it might be better if we returned to Vushta and the Western Kingdoms with all due speed. Even though Mother Duck appears to be fighting our battle, we still have a war."

Norei was right, and I told her so. We would leave as soon as all our party had gathered together.

The dwarves and His Brownieship were already here. The beating of a drum heralded the arrival of Guxx and Brax, and Snarks arrived shortly thereafter, complaining about the conditions of his robes. There was a flapping of wings overhead, and Hubert landed in the middle of the clearing, Alea astride his back. The unicorn galloped into our midst and proceeded to gaze moodily in my direction. Hendrek was next, using his great warclub to smash through the underbrush. I saw, as he approached, that he carried Tap upon his shoulder. And, fast upon his heels, I heard a joyous eeping as my ferret bounded forth to greet me.

We were almost all here, then. All save my master. But where was Ebenezum? Where might he have hidden when he gave up the shoe?

There was a rustling in the bushes behind me.

"Master?" I called.

But it was not Ebenezum, but instead Jeffrey who skulked into our midst.

"Anybody know of any openings for talking wolves?" he asked hopefully.

I had no time to answer his query. I looked down at His Brownieship.

"But where is my master?"

A wind as cold as winter sprung up before His Smallness could answer. I spun about as I heard that familiar dry chuckle. But why would he be here now, when all my companions were about me?

I looked into the face of Death.

"Greetings," the spectre whispered, the sound of snow falling over frozen tundra. "I usually don't speak before such a large audience. At least not an audience of the living."

Norei grabbed my arm. "What are you doing here?" she demanded. "There are too many of us. You cannot take Wuntvor now!"

"I do not need Wuntvor—now." Death grinned. "I have another new addition to my kingdom." He paused, and stared straight at me. "A wizardly addition."

"My master?" I blurted.

Death nodded. "The wizard Ebenezum. I found him, all alone in the forest. But he has joined me now."

"No!" I screamed. "You cannot take him!"

The spectre shrugged. "True, it is not yet his time. But Death takes who he wants, when he wants."

I could stand no more of this. With a scream of rage I drew my sword and ran for the spectre.

Death did not move, except to extend his hands toward me. He laughed at my approach, the sound of thunder above a forest fire.

I stopped, realizing that even now I dared not risk the spectre's touch. Killing myself would not save my master.

"You hesitate?" Death asked. "Then perhaps we can

negotiate. The wizard might yet again walk the earth. I would
release his soul on certain conditions."

The spectre pointed a single bone-white finger at me.

"I would consider a trade."

"Wuntvor! No!" Norei cried.

"Oh, I don't want to be hasty about this thing," Death quickly
added. "I will let the Eternal Apprentice consider his options.
Remember, Death has all the time in the world. When you are
ready, Wuntvor, all you have to do is say my name."

The spectre vanished, his laughter hanging in the air for a
moment before it, too, faded away.

I turned back to the others. Death had my master. What
should I do?

My companions were talking all around me. Norei looked
at me, her face full of concern. She might have asked me a
question. I did not know.

All I could hear was Death's laughter, ringing in my ears.

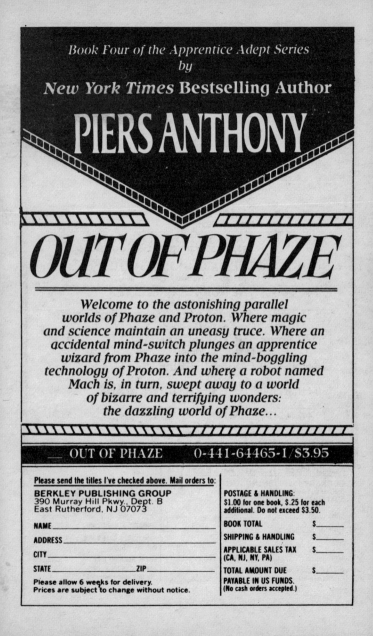

Book Four of the Apprentice Adept Series
by

New York Times Bestselling Author

PIERS ANTHONY

OUT OF PHAZE

*Welcome to the astonishing parallel
worlds of Phaze and Proton. Where magic
and science maintain an uneasy truce. Where an
accidental mind-switch plunges an apprentice
wizard from Phaze into the mind-boggling
technology of Proton. And where a robot named
Mach is, in turn, swept away to a world
of bizarre and terrifying wonders:
the dazzling world of Phaze...*

___ OUT OF PHAZE   0-441-64465-1/$3.95